AVENGING
THE OWL

Melissa Hart

To the Rausch kids,
from one animal lover
to three others.
Enjoy!
Melissa Hart

Sky Pony Press
NEW YORK

Sky Pony Press books may be purchased in bulk at special discounts for sales promotion, corporate gifts, fund-raising, or educational purposes. Special editions can also be created to specifications. For details, contact the Special Sales Department, Sky Pony Press, 307 West 36th Street, 11th Floor, New York, NY 10018 or info@skyhorsepublishing.com.

Sky Pony® is a registered trademark of Skyhorse Publishing, Inc.®, a Delaware corporation.

Visit our website at www.skyponypress.com.

10 9 8 7 6 5 4 3 2 1

Library of Congress Cataloging-in-Publication Data is available on file.

ISBN: 978-1-63450-147-7
Ebook ISBN: 978-1-63450-610-6

Cover design by Sarah Brody
Cover image credit Stephen Mulcahey / Arcangel

Printed in the United States of America

For Maia, who loves the Earth

CONTENTS

CHAPTER ONE
RAPTOR MEANS TO SEIZE

According to Mr. Davies's junior high screenwriting class, the word means *payback*. But avenge is more than plain old revenge. Avenge is a word that yanks you to your feet—heart pounding and palms prickling with sweat—to root for the hero. It's a word about justice.

In that old B movie, *Them!*, Sergeant Ben Peterson avenges the death of a little girl's family by destroying the nest of giant mutating ants that slaughtered them. A long time ago, in a galaxy far, far away, Han Solo avenged the destruction of an innocent planet by helping Luke Skywalker blow up the Death Star.

Sergeant Ben got away without being killed by mammoth ants. Han got a gold medal from a beautiful princess with really weird hair. But when I avenged the murder of the only thing that mattered to me, I got eight weeks cleaning poop off birdcages.

1

My new social worker told me I'd have to show up at the raptor place at the base of the mountain every single morning, no matter what. Forced labor, like those guys in the orange suits they let out of jail to pick up bottles and bags along the freeway. Only I'd be working with birds instead of trash.

I almost told my social worker no way. Throw me in the hole; give me a month in solitary over caring for a bunch of hawks. But then I remembered how my father had hung his head in the courtroom when the judge proclaimed his straight-A son a full-fledged At-Risk Youth. Dad went all pale and sick, looking ready to crawl back into his striped pajamas for another six weeks.

If he hadn't already ruined my life, he would've broken my heart right then.

·

"Well . . . guess I'm off." I stalked into the kitchen on my first day of community service and felt the trailer sway beneath my feet. I scowled at the orange flowered linoleum and glanced over at Dad. Maybe he'd take pity on me, give me a reprieve when he saw me in my oldest, rattiest clothes like a version of Oliver Twist.

"Be careful." Dad hunched over the newspaper at the kitchen table without looking up.

I grabbed a banana from the fruit bowl and bailed, slamming the trailer's joke of a screen door behind me. "You be careful, too," I muttered.

That first morning, Mom gave me a ride to the Raptor Rescue Center. It took about a year for her purple Volkswagen bus to chug up the mountain road past the endless evergreen trees. Right as the bus almost blew a gasket rounding a curve, I named it The Big Grape. A lot rides on a name, and this one fit perfectly.

"This rig sucks." I folded my arms tight across my ancient Rip Curl T-shirt and glared out the window. My pencil jabbed my butt through my shorts. I yanked it out of my back pocket and stuck it behind my ear. Mr. Davies always had a pencil behind his ear and a notebook in his pocket, in case inspiration struck and he had to scribble down a screenplay on the fly.

Did he miss me yet?

"You've got what it takes to be a writer, Solo," he said on the last day of seventh grade. We stood outside after the graduation ceremony with the mist creeping up from the ocean, both of us in suits and ties. He put a hand on my shoulder. "Promise me you'll keep working on those screenplays. Make your dreams come true."

Dreams. I snorted, perched on the hard front seat of the ridiculous Volkswagen bus with exhaust in my nostrils. My life had become one big nightmare.

Mom shoved the accelerator to the floor. The Big Grape groaned in pain, bucking past a mailbox and straight up a super-steep hill. We pulled into a parking area beside some pavilion with a bunch of benches and lurched to a stop inches away from a tree.

"We're here!" Mom's smile worked overtime.

"*Wonderful.*" I stared out the window at a couple of blue-walled porta potties under more trees.

"What's happened to you?" Mom's smile vanished, and she morphed into Disapproving Maternal Character. "You used to be such a little gentleman. I don't even know you anymore."

I shot her the sideways evil eye. "I don't know you, either."

My mother wore ugly, chunky sandals under a long, swirly, blue and white skirt. She'd yard-saled her board shorts and her bikini; I wondered if she'd sold her diamond earrings, too. She looked like a hippie from the 1960s, all dressed up to sing and dance in Golden Gate Park . . . except for the warning look that flashed in her eyes. "Don't be snarky, Solo."

"Sorry." I picked at the ancient stuffing spilling out of a rip in my seat. "But why'd we have to sell the Corvette? This bus is humiliating."

Mom closed her eyes. "That Corvette was nothing but a status symbol."

"You sound like Dad." I unclipped my seatbelt, the better to turn around fully and glare at her. "What the heck's a status symbol?"

"It's something you own so other people will think you've . . ." She twirled a strand of sandy hair around her finger, searching for the right words. "Made it."

"We *had* made it, Mom. That Corvette was a sweet ride."

"You know perfectly well why I couldn't drive that car after your father . . ."

Mom's voice died, and she stared hard at something over my shoulder. I glanced behind me. A tall woman with a head of wild red hair loped toward us in jeans and green high-top sneakers. A bird the size of a Coke bottle perched on her gloved hand, ruffling his feathers in a blur of blue-gray-brown-black-rust-white.

My mother recovered her voice and her smile. "I think that's your boss."

"*Jailer*'s more like it. She's a prison warden."

Mom's jaw tightened. "Get out and introduce yourself. Don't embarrass me."

I rolled my eyes and heaved myself out of The Big Grape with my backpack held in front of me in case the bird decided to attack.

The woman stretched out her hand. "I'm Minerva," she said, low and gravelly. "This," she nodded at the bird on her wrist, "is Cyclops."

Minerva's voice gripped me, as relentless as her handshake, and forced me to acknowledge her sidekick. The bird flapped its wings, but stayed put on her arm. I squinted. Thin straps around his feet went to a hook that clipped to her glove.

"Cyclops is a kestrel—North America's smallest falcon." Minerva nodded at the bird's right eye, scrunched tight in a permanent wink. "He's partially blind."

I'd never seen a bird this close up, not even a seagull on the beach back home. Its tiny beak curved like a fishhook and eight little sharp talons dug into the leather glove.

"It's good to meet you." My mother got out of the bus and clasped Minerva's hand.

The kestrel flapped again. He peered at me out of his good eye and chirped. "Thank you for agreeing to help Solo," Mom continued. "He really is a good—"

"The way I understand it," Minerva's voice interrupted smoothly, "Solo is helping us. Follow me."

She strode up the driveway toward a lawn surrounded by trees with trunks thick as Monster Truck tires. Shadowy creatures lurked inside tall screened cages all around me. Suddenly, a creature somewhere above let out an ear-piercing shriek.

Ki ki ki ki kee!

I ducked and covered my head.

Caw! Caw!

"What the . . . ?" I leaped back, shaking in my sports sandals, and took shelter under a tree hung with bird feeders.

"It gets pretty loud around here." Minerva's voice remained calm, like we weren't standing smack in the middle of Alfred Hitchcock's horror movie *The Birds*. "We rehabilitate sick and injured raptors, but some don't recover well enough to be released into the wild. When that happens, we can often find homes for them. Some of them end up staying here."

My mother nodded and pressed her palms together against her chest, bowing slightly in some show of hippie-gratitude for Minerva's mission. I rolled my eyes.

"That's fascinating," Mom breathed. "This is a silly question, I know, but what exactly *is* a raptor?"

She reached out an arm to pull me into the conversation. I moved away from her, still searching for a safe spot to get away from the birds.

Minerva nodded at Cyclops, who gripped her wrist even tighter with his evil little talons. "The word *raptor* means *to seize.*"

My hand flew to the bandage on my left wrist, testing for pain. *I could roll down the hill below us and vanish into the trees. They'd never find me. I'd hitchhike back to California and . . .*

"You might want to listen to this, Solo. It's important information to know if you're going to volunteer here. Visitors might come up to you with questions." Minerva raised one eyebrow. "Raptors hunt with their talons, grabbing their prey with them. Then they use their beak to rip their prey apart. Let me put Cyclops in his enclosure and I'll show you our peregrine falcon. Their hunting technique is fascinating."

Minerva led Mom toward a cage. I stood rigid on the lawn. I already knew all about the way raptors hunt— had seen it up close and personal. The sun boiled the top of my head. All around me, sparrow-looking things twittered in the trees, flaunting their freedom high above the caged raptors. I thought about my friends out surfing back home and punted a small rock. It crashed down the hill and the bird near me screamed and flew back and forth, hitting the sides of its cage.

My mother's voice drifted toward me. I caught the words *shotgun* and *disabled boy* before I slunk away in disgust to a spot where she couldn't see me.

"Oh, well," a voice beside me croaked. "Ha ha ha ha!"

I peered into a flower garden. Yellow butterflies floated into the trees. A squirrel curled its gray tail like a windsurfer's sail, bawling out some blue bird on a feeder.

"Well?" the voice said again. "Ha ha ha ha!"

I spun around and stared into the nearest cage. A crow as black as my hair sat on a perch.

"Did you . . . did you laugh?" I stammered, real quiet. Too many loony tunes in my family already. No one needed to know I was talking to birds.

The crow cocked its head and looked at me sideways out of one shiny black eye. "Well?"

"You *talk*?"

Minerva crunched down the gravel path and pointed at a laminated sign near the cage, packed with information and a picture of the bird. "This is Edgar Allen Crow," she said.

Mom whooped like it was the funniest joke she'd ever heard. "That's wonderful! Just like the poet. You know, sweetie, Edgar Allen *Poe*." She turned to Minerva.

"Solo's father reads Poe's poem *The Raven* out loud to us every Halloween."

Minerva pointed with a bandaged index finger. "The raven's in the next mew. Her name is Hephaestus."

An even bigger black bird with a long, curved beak flipped its head backward and looked at me upside down. "What're you doing?" it demanded.

Mom clapped her hands. "This one speaks, too! Do all raptors talk?"

Her voice was giving me a headache. Beside me, Minerva massaged her temples with her fingers. Did she have a headache, too? Lately, it seemed like Mom never stopped talking and always in a high-pitched, frantic voice that made me want to walk around with wax plugs permanently stuck into my ears.

Mom and I used to be friends, surfing buddies, both of us heading out at 6:00 a.m. with our boards. But then, she'd turned enemy.

"Edgar and Hephaestus aren't raptors." Minerva plucked a long black feather from the ground and stuck it in the back pocket of her dirty jeans. "They're corvids I rescued years ago."

Mom peered into a food dish in the raven's cage. "Is that tofu?"

"Yup. In the wild, they'd eat small birds and rodents. Here, they get cat food, fruit, and chunks of tofu."

"Hear that, Solo?" Mom elbowed my side. I ducked my head, blocking her from my vision. Tofu was another one of my mother's new instruments of torture. I hated the white spongy squares she cooked with rice or tried to hide in vegetarian chili. "Bean curd," she regularly sang out in the trailer's cramped, dark kitchen. "Nutritious and delicious!"

I tried to choke the stuff down at dinner. As I spit it out into my napkin, all I could think of was that nursery rhyme:

> *Little Miss Muffet*
> *Sat on a tuffet,*
> *Eating her curds and whey;*
> *Along came a spider,*
> *Who sat down beside her,*
> *And frightened Miss Muffet away.*

I swear, I'd eat a spider any day over some bean curd that—from the looks of Hephaestus's food dish—even a raven wouldn't eat.

"Solo, I'd like to introduce you to the other birds," Minerva continued.

I looked up to find my mother walking back to the bus. Minerva tapped her sneaker impatiently against the gravel, a crease between her eyebrows.

"Well?" Edgar said.

I backed away. That crow gave me the creeps. "They're all in cages, right?"

"The proper term for a bird enclosure is a *mew*."

"Great." The sun gripped the back of my neck. I shoved my sunglasses down on my nose and shuffled behind her.

"This is a northern harrier." She pointed to a bird with a long tail. "They make their nests on the ground. Hers got destroyed by a haying machine, and she lost part of her wing."

The harrier bent to pick at something dead on the ground—something with gray fur. My stomach lurched. I ground my teeth together, praying I wouldn't throw up.

Minerva moved to another mew. A blue tarp stretched across the bottom half, three feet tall. "That's Artemis." She braced her hands on her hips. "Never, ever go into her mew. She's sitting on eggs, and it makes her moody. Let's move on so we don't disturb her."

A grouchy bird. I bent and peeked through a rip in the tarp—nothing but gravel and a brown and white feather.

Minerva consulted her silver wristwatch with an owl on its face. She pushed her hair behind her ears, revealing silver owl earrings that glimmered. In a screenplay, Mr. Davies would have described her as a Hard-Core Bird Nerd . . . I just knew it. "I've got a preschool class coming for a tour at eleven," she said. "I'll tell you Artemis's story later."

I shrugged, then stopped dead in front of a giant mew that loomed twenty feet high. There sat two of the biggest birds I'd ever seen—tall as kindergartners, white heads gleaming above dark bodies.

"Those are the bald eagles," said Minerva. They sat up on long perches, straight and dignified, twin presidents behind wire.

"They're huge!"

At the sound of my voice, one eagle screamed and flapped to the other side of the mew.

"Keep your voice low," Minerva hissed. "Never, *ever* yell at a raptor."

"*Sorry*." I stuffed my hands in my pockets and clamped my lips shut.

Minerva lowered herself onto a wooden bench and dropped her head into her hands, massaging her temples again. She didn't want me working for her—I knew it.

If she fires me, will I have to go to jail?

Above us, the more chilled out eagle lifted a foot and arched it like he was doing bicep curls.

"What . . . what's he doing *that* for?"

"He's relaxing." Minerva flexed her ankles in green socks speckled with black bird silhouettes, and the line in her forehead softened.

Kik ik ik! The crazy eagle cackled from a far perch and spread its wings wide.

"Let's leave them alone now."

I gripped the bandage around my wrist and stumbled after Minerva down a path and past a redheaded vulture hunched over a tennis ball in its mew. "That's Xerxes." She straightened a sign clipped to the wire. "He likes to untie people's shoelaces."

She pointed at two big rust-colored birds side by side on a perch in another mew. "Red-tailed hawks," she said. "Both female, inseparable."

She marched me down past even more mews, through a wooden gate and then another, and we stopped at a little blue-roofed building. She opened a screen door and led me into a room. "The clinic," she said. "We prepare food here and treat birds in there." She pointed through another screen door at a room with a tall metal examination table. From another room, I heard a man's voice saying something about fresh rabbits for the eagles.

A smell assaulted my nostrils, cold and raw like fresh meat. Syringes and scissors littered the clinic's countertop. Metal pie pans smeared with blood and feathers crowded the sink. On one shelf, I saw a tray full of yellow baby chicks, all dead. On another, a plate of lifeless mice—brown bodies lined up like sausages. Only the desk was clear—just a computer, keyboard, and a sleeping bundle of black and brown feathers. *Uncaged.*

My heart stopped.

"This is Hermes." Minerva clucked her tongue against her teeth.

Instantly, the bundle leaped to its feet. Talons shone black against an Astroturf-covered two-by-four. Feathers rose into horns on the bird's bobbing head, and I found myself face-to-face with my archenemy: a great horned owl.

"I can't work here," I said and bolted out the door.

CHAPTER TWO
OWLS = DEATH

WHOO-*hoo-oo-oo-oo*-WHOO-WHOO!
The sound yanked my hair on end. I sprinted blindly down a path and fell over a log. Minerva found me slumped on a bench beside a rusty windmill, nursing a bloody toenail and two scraped knees.

"What're you doing?" With her chest all puffed out, she looked like one of her raptors. I stared at the owls on her green sweatshirt. Different kinds of owls, all with round sinister eyes staring into mine.

"I hate birds!" I hurled a rock, and it rolled through the tangle of blackberries to a trail far below.

Minerva examined a tiny black and white bird twittering on the branch of some white-berried bush. She reached into her pocket and tossed a handful of seed in its direction. Then she said, "Lots of people dislike owls. Some Native Americans regard them as bad luck. In fact, tribes in the Northwest believe owls call out the names of people who are about to die."

"Owls equal death," I muttered. "I could've told you that."

A montage of scenes whirled through my head. Huge, flapping wings. Razor-sharp beak. Bloody talons. The crack of a single gunshot. I dug my palms into my eyes.

"They don't always equal death, although great horned owls *are* at the top of the food chain." The bench trembled as Minerva sat down beside me. "Anyhow, I heard about your kitten. I'm sorry."

I snorted. People always say they're sorry when a stranger dies or ends up in the hospital. I hate that. No one but me knew how my kitten loved to snuggle under the covers, purring against my chest, or how she woke me every morning practically tearing the skin off my ear with her scratchy tongue. No one but me knew that at eight o'clock every night, she chased the blue plastic ring from a milk carton across my bedroom floor and batted it around for an hour like a fluffy gray and white soccer forward.

How could Minerva be sorry?

The long, sad wail of a train drifted up from the city below. Minerva's eyes followed a black and yellow butterfly floating above the flowers. We had monarchs in my old town, orange as the kites my friends and I used to fly at the beach before my parents sold our house and forced me to move with them into a trailer in Oregon.

Minerva shifted her gaze from the butterfly to me. "Owls seldom kill cats unless they're desperate for food." She pursed her lips. "Or unless someone's invaded their territory."

I snorted again. My parents' tin can trailer didn't invade anyone's territory. There were billions of places a great horned owl could've found a meal on their new property. But what was the point of arguing? My kitten was dead.

And I was here.

A gray squirrel raced up a tree beside us and bumped into a brown squirrel. They cursed at each other in Rodent Speak, practically pelting each other with acorns. They reminded me of the cartoons my father used to write in Hollywood—of a life that seemed so far away now.

I hurled another rock down the hill. "Watch out, squirrels. You're owl bait."

Minerva studied me. "Your social worker sent you to the raptor center for a reason."

I lifted my chin and met her eyes.

She reached out and touched the bandage on my wrist, tapping it gently with her own wrapped-up index finger. "I'd like you to come and meet Hermes properly. I'll put him in his inside mew."

It was a command, not an invitation. Minerva stood and reached to help me up from the bench, but I ignored her hand, pretending to be fascinated with the mew beside me. Inside sat two tiny owls, motionless as stuffed toys on a branch.

"Pygmy owls." Minerva clucked her tongue at them. "Our smallest. They camouflage beautifully with that oak perch. . . ."

The brownish pygmies were smaller than my hand. Still, their talons looked sharp enough to pluck out my eyes like the crows did to that teacher-woman in *The Birds*.

I turned my back on the mew and stalked across the grass.

"Well?" Edgar cried. "Ha ha ha ha!"

I glared at the creepy crow. "Save it, featherbrain."

Outside the death room, Minerva pulled on an elbow-length leather glove. "Wait here," she instructed. Through the window, I saw her nudge the glove under Hermes's feet on the desk. Now, I could see the brown leash clipped from his ankle to the perch. She unclipped it, and the owl hopped up onto her wrist. I held my breath, sure the bird would rip her face in two. But Hermes just sat there.

Minerva guided him to a perch inside a small mew against the wall, then shut the door. "You can come in now, Solo."

I shuffled inside, eyes glued on Hermes. He stared back at me, bobbing his head from side to side, twin head-feather tufts on high alert.

"Why's he doing that? Does he want to eat me?"

Minerva shook her head. "It's called motion parallax. He pins you in his vision by keeping what's behind you moving. You're right—it's a hunting technique, but you're too big to be prey. Try it yourself."

18

She held up her finger. "Pretend your finger's a mouse. Stare at it, and keep it still, then move your head from side to side. See how this helps you to focus on your finger?"

She was watching, so I had to try. The trick reminded me of seagulls floating on the ocean back home. The water all around them moved, but the birds looked perfectly still.

"Why's Hermes here?" I demanded. "He looks healthy."

"Injured wing." Minerva picked up a brown and white striped feather from the desk and ran her finger over it. "He fell out of the nest when he was a baby and broke his wing, so he can't fly properly. He helps with education when school groups come to visit. Which reminds me, I'd better get moving. The kids'll be here any minute."

The phone jangled across the office. Hermes let out a hoot and flapped his wings. One of them dangled crookedly at his side.

Phone tucked between her ear and shoulder, Minerva opened the mew door and set a pink tennis shoe inside. Instantly, Hermes pounced and gripped the thing in both feet, attacking it with his beak. He ripped off a piece of pink canvas and tossed it aside. I cringed.

"Injured hawk?" Minerva said into the phone. "Near which highway? We'll send someone." She covered the mouthpiece with her hand. "I've gotta call volunteers to pick up a hawk. Change the poopy newspaper in Hermes's mew and give him a snack."

"A snack?" I looked around for some Goldfish crackers or an apple. Minerva pointed to a plate on top of the refrigerator. In the center lay a dead white mouse.

"You're kidding, right?" My stomach went belly-up. My best friend, Rajen, had two pet mice back home—cute little guys with pink wriggling noses and whiskers that tickled your face. "*Gross!*" No way was I touching a dead mouse.

Minerva hung up the phone. "Is it any grosser than people eating sausage and steak and fried chicken? Life feeds on life, Solo. Get used to it."

I shook my head. "My mom's gone vegetarian. We eat tofu."

"Well, Hermes is an obligate carnivore. He has to eat meat, or he'll die." She handed me the plate and peered into my face.

"You're not scared of a three-pound bird, are you?" She picked up the phone again and turned her back on me. "Hi, Lucas. It's Minerva. We've got an injured hawk. . . ."

I peered into the mew. Slimy black and white bird poop dotted the newspapers. Hermes sat on his tennis shoe, another fragment of the canvas in his killer beak.

"Hurry up, Solo. We've got a lot to do this morning." Minerva tossed me her leather glove. "That's an *order*."

I thought of what the judge had told me that day in court: *Next time, you won't be so lucky.*

Heart pounding, I pulled on the glove and opened the mew door, yanked out the newspapers, and slammed the door shut. Even with my breath held, the tall metal trash can smelled like death. Among crumpled newspapers, I saw a pair of orange chicken feet with no body.

I squinted at the mouse on the plate. Somehow, I had to get it into the mew without losing my hand or my breakfast. Minerva sat on the desk with her back to me, chattering away. I snatched up the plate and some newspapers, opened the mew door, and shoved in the stack of newspaper with the rodent on top.

Bam! I closed the door just in time. Hermes hooted and jumped to his perch, ear tufts jutting. He stared down at his mouse on the messy pile of newspaper and clacked his beak.

"He'll sit up there a while and contemplate his snack." Minerva stepped toward the door. "Then he'll eat it. Lucas may bring in an injured hawk—help him with whatever he needs. I'm gonna gulp down a quick bowl of soup myself before the school group gets here. That's where I live." She pointed out the window at a building beside the clinic.

"Wonderful." I poked at a white splotch with my hand still hot in her glove. Owl poop on my shirt.

"It *is* wonderful. I get to listen to owls hooting all night. You can fold these towels." Minerva nodded at a basket on the counter piled high with white towels. "Put 'em in the treatment room cabinets when you're finished. You'll see a lot of plastic crates draped with sheets in that room. We cover them so recently injured birds can have peace and quiet."

I looked at the clock. 10:40 a.m. Three hours before I could escape. "You're leaving me alone in here?"

"The birds are all enclosed. Besides, I wouldn't leave you if I didn't think you could handle it. Thanks for being here, Solo."

I rolled my eyes. Why thank me? I had to work here—the judge said so.

Minerva walked out of the office, then turned back and pulled a paperback from a stack near the desk. She dropped it on top of my backpack. "You might like this."

I looked at the cover—a great horned owl hunched on a fallen log, glaring at the camera. No way was I reading that book.

Minerva left me then, and I got busy with the towels, one eye on Hermes in case he decided to attack. But he just kept staring at his mouse like he wished it would wake up and give him a chase.

Suddenly, an eerie wail drifted out of the treatment room.

WHOO-hoo-oo-oo-oo-WHOO-WHOO!

Then, Hermes started bobbing his head like crazy. Goosebumps prickled my back and shivered down my arms. I twisted a towel between my hands. Minerva had ordered me to put them in some cabinet in the treatment room. I folded and refolded, stalling for time.

I'll run in, dump the towels, and get out. She said they were all locked up . . .

WHOO-hoo-oo-oo-oo-WHOO-WHOO!

With my arms full of terry cloth rectangles, I creaked through the screen door and tiptoed into the dim room, found the cabinet marked TOWELS, and stuffed them in. Something rustled inside the biggest plastic crate. The sheet didn't quite cover the door, and I glimpsed two round yellow eyes peering at me through the wire.

Another owl. It lunged for me, slamming against metal.

WHOO-hoo-oo-oo-oo-WHOO-WHOO!

This time, the hooting came from the clinic.

I ran out of the treatment room and stared at Hermes. He'd forgotten all about his breakfast. Now he stood tall and thin on his perch, calling out to the injured owl.

My head swam with hooting. I shouldered my backpack and ran for the door. A book hit the ground—the paperback Minerva had given me. I stuffed it inside my pack and fled.

What am I supposed to do now?

Minerva had disappeared, probably off eating mouse muffins with peanut butter. Shaking, I slid down to the driveway outside the clinic and leaned against the wall. I reached into my backpack for a photo—a picture of me and Blinky and my best friend, Rajen—all of us in wet suits in front of the Redondo Beach Pier. I turned the photo over and read Rajen's yellow sticky note.

Hey, dude.

*The waves rock! We surfed ten-footers
today. Blinky says hi. I'm fixing up my
tree house. Don't forget Operation Surf's Up!*

*Your friend,
Rajen*

I sniffed the photo. I could almost smell the ocean, feel the sun hot on my shoulders, cool blue waves lifting me up and carrying me away from this horrible place.

WHOO-hoo-oo-oo-oo-WHOO-WHOO! called the owl from the treatment room, and Hermes answered. I stood up and peered through the window into the clinic. Sunlight pushed through the miniblinds, striping the room with shadowy bars. The owls kept hooting back and forth. Their cries twisted in my chest and caught in my throat.

All at once, I knew what they were saying.

I want to go home.

CHAPTER THREE

SAY GOOD-BYE TO HOLLYWOOD

Labels are important. They show you where to file things in your head so you can stay organized. "Owls" get filed under DEATH. File "Fathers" under CRAZY. "Kids" go into the file marked POWERLESS.

In *The Blob*, two teenagers try to warn everyone that a giant mass of jelly from another planet is murdering humans, but no one listens to them. By the time people realize the kids are telling the truth, half the town is dead. No one can believe a couple of teens could be heroes.

"*You're* going to be a hero, just like your namesake," Mom used to tell me. I loved that story about how, when Mom was a kid, her mother took her to see *Star Wars* at Grauman's Chinese Theatre in Los Angeles, and she fell in love with the hero, Han Solo. And since Dad's last name is Hahn, she thought it would be cute to name me Solo.

Solo Hahn—can you believe it? What Mom forgot is that "Solo" gets filed under ALONE . . . *Solitary.* I'm nobody's hero. Still, good thing she liked *Star Wars* instead of some other movie from her childhood. Otherwise, my friends might be calling me E. T.

My parents make no sense, really. If they were characters in one of my screenplays, they'd have tons of asides, talking right to the camera so the audience would know what they were thinking while their son wandered around clueless.

Here's what my father said to me one Saturday last May, right as I was walking out the door with my surfboard:

"Solo, we're moving to Oregon. Pack up your necessities, and leave all superfluous frivolities behind."

"*What?*"

"Contemplate your belongings." Dad shuffled down the hall in his squashed leather slippers. "Decide what you can't live without."

"Wait! What the heck are you talking about?"

Dad had studied creative writing in college. Big words and bigger ideas flooded his sentences. I had to wade through a whole sea of them before I finally understood three things:

#1. My father was a mess. For a month, he'd been laying around in his striped pajamas, watching old horror movies on his 60-inch flat screen TV. His favorite was *Attack of the Killer Tomatoes*—these three crazy guys launch a siege against a bunch of fruit that's been eating people and pets. One morning, Dad appeared on the beach with a robe wrapped around him and told Mom and me, just in from surfing, that even though he brought home mammoth paychecks, he was sick of writing cartoons.

"But I can't afford to follow my heart," he told us. "Novelists don't make money unless they're that *Da Vinci Code* guy."

We thought it was a phase until that night, when he got into Mom's Corvette and tried to leave us. We foiled his escape plan; he countered by quitting his job.

"I thought you couldn't afford to follow your heart," I said.

His eyes got all spacey then. "Maybe . . ." From the deck of his bedroom, he stared out toward the ocean. "Maybe I can't afford *not* to."

That's when I knew he'd gone crazy. He informed us that he'd decided to devote his time to writing a novel about Japanese internment during World War II because his parents spent a year locked up and he wanted to "honor the memory of their struggle."

#2. He got my mother to quit *her* job as a history teacher at El Camino College. "Don't look at me like that, Solo," she said. "We have enough in savings to live on for a year. We'll be fine."

Right after that, she tossed a half-full box of Hostess cupcakes and a can of grape Kool-Aid mix into the trash. When I asked why she'd glugged a whole liter of Coke down the kitchen sink, she told me, "Sugar causes anxiety, and your father's had all he can stand."

#3. My parents put our two-story beach house up for sale so they could buy an acre of land and a double-wide trailer a thousand miles north in the middle of Oregon, an hour away from an ocean so cold the fish freeze. Dad showed me a picture of our new "house." It looked like a can of Spam.

"It's sixteen hours away from Redondo Beach!" I hollered.

He nodded. "Exactly."

Then, I understood one more thing. I was really, really mad. If I were a character in one of my father's cartoons, steam would've spouted from my ears. My hair would've burst into flames. My eyeballs would've popped out of their sockets and bounced around on the floor.

"I'm not moving!" I burst into the master bedroom, frothing at the mouth. "You can't make me!"

My parents traded a look over my head—one of those loaded stares the camera loves, where the eyes say it all.

"We know it'll be hard on you to leave your friends. . . ." My mother reached to hug me.

I jerked my head away so she ended up kissing air. "It's not hard, 'cause I'm not leaving!"

"Our house is up for sale." My father's voice came out stern, but his eyes were dark pools of saltwater behind his wire-rimmed glasses. "This way, we can spend more time together. I barely know you, Solo."

I'd give him that. For years, Dad had caught the carpool to Los Angeles before dawn. He didn't get back until after dinner. Sometimes, he worked weekends. He'd come home and rip off his tie like it was strangling him, then collapse on the leather couch in front of the TV. Some days we said about two words to each other. But late at night, he would tiptoe to my door and stand there looking at me. He thought I was sleeping. He couldn't see my eyes slivered open, trying to read his face in the dark. I never fell asleep until he'd gone.

"Oh, Solo." Since I wasn't accepting any hugs just then, Mom crossed the bedroom and put her arms around Dad. Her voice came out all shaky. "I miss Oregon. I grew up there, sweetie. It will be a much simpler, happier life."

"We have a fine life right here in Redondo Beach!" I screamed.

That year, I'd been vice president of the seventh-grade student council, and the principal put me in GATE— Gifted and Talented Education—which meant Rajen and I went to a special class every Wednesday morning. We designed our own board games, read *Reader's Digest* to old people in the retirement home next door, and the Toastmasters people taught us to give speeches about how we shouldn't have homework and the cafeteria should always serve pizza.

After school, there was surfing. Some guys my age loved girls or video games. I loved the ocean. I understood it, and it understood me. My fingers gripped the board as a wave began to rise far out at sea. The water gathered momentum, and my heart began to pound. I squinted through golden sunlight, studying the swell. Right as it crested and roared, I turned, leaped onto my board, and rode the long, long wave into shore.

I stopped surfing when the sign appeared, nailed to a post in our front yard. Sold.

Then, even the fishy smell of seaweed made me want to bawl like a first grader. But there was enough saltwater in the Pacific already.

•

Right after school got out that summer, my parents had a mammoth yard sale. People swarmed over our stuff like ants over spilled Coke. Mom walked into my bedroom and clicked off my stereo, then stood in front of the TV. "We're selling the television." She glanced at my notebooks full of screenplays, my surfing trophies, piles of CDs and DVDs.

"That's okay. Dad can watch mine." I waved her out of the way, but she didn't budge.

"We're selling *all* the televisions. We're going to be a TV-free household."

I stared at her. She wore her designer jeans and the diamond earrings Dad had given her for their anniversary, but she'd traded her Hollywood hairdo for braids—*Little House on the Prairie*-style. With those braids, she looked as young as one of the senior girls at what was supposed to be my new high school in a little more than a year.

"How'm I supposed to watch movies?" I demanded. "You're joking, right?"

Mom pursed up her lips, deadly serious. "There's a lovely little theater in our new city in an old converted church. We can go all the time. You might as well sell your DVDs, too, and save the money for something you really need."

What I needed was for this to be some freaky tilt shot in the fictional film noir screenplay of my life. But it was real. "In living color," as Dad would say.

"I can't believe you're doing this!" I shouted.

I grabbed my box of DVDs and thrust it into her hands. "Happy now?" Then, I ripped the TV plug out of its socket. Orange sparks shot everywhere.

My parents had turned into aliens with ray guns on a mission to annihilate my life. There went my TV— *Bzzzt!* There went surfing—*Bzzzt!* There went my friends—*Bzzzt!* and *Bzzzt!*

"Solo, can you tone down the murderous glare?" Mom glanced out at Dad washing the lower windows of the house. "You know why we have to move. The doctor says your father needs a change, and you and I just have to . . ." The doorbell rang and she sprinted down the hall to answer it.

A minute later, Rajen clumped up the stairs. "What's up with your mom, dude? She looks totally bizarre. Where's she taking your DVDs?"

"Don't ask." It hurt to look at my best friend. Instead, I stared out the window while strangers below began to cart off everything that meant something to me—my movies, our huge stereo, even our computer.

"That stinks you gotta sell your stuff." Rajen smashed his face against the window, freaking out some woman walking off with my mother's makeup mirror. "Bet you're making a pile of cash on your garage sale."

"It's a *yard* sale." Thanks to my father, we weren't allowed to use the garage anymore.

Dad wandered upstairs to get my TV. "Hey, Rajen," he said, then looked at me and opened his mouth like he wanted to say something. Then he hung his head and skulked out of the room with his skinny arms wrapped around my flat screen, trailing the cord behind him. Bad sign. He was never tongue-tied before he got sick.

"No way," Rajen said. "You're selling *your* TV?"

I shrugged. "We're getting a plasma screen after we move."

"Cool!" He flipped through a pile of surfing magazines. "Is your new house in Oregon as awesome as this one?"

"Yeah." Even best friends don't tell each other everything. "But soon as we get to Oregon, I'm running away. I'll be back in a couple of weeks."

Rajen nodded. "You can sleep in my tree house. Hey, bro, how much for these magazines?"

"Just take 'em." I threw my pillow across the room. It clattered one of my trophies into the trash can. "Count it toward rent on the tree house."

After Rajen left, I stomped out to the front yard. My mother stood in the driveway, packing up the stuff that hadn't sold. Boxes littered the lawn. "We'll donate all this to Goodwill. It'll go to someone in need."

"*I'm* someone in need." I grabbed my Dodgers hat before she could toss it. "I need new parents."

This was grounds for a lecture on what my mother called Voluntary Simplicity. "We actually need so little, Solo." She folded old beach towels and dropped them into a box. "The Native Americans existed beautifully on just three things—food, water, and shelters they made themselves out of sticks and animal skins."

I knew better than to argue with her when she got all historical. I slumped on a box and studied the things our neighbors hadn't wanted. Literature textbooks. Ancient cassette tapes of Dad's big band music. My *Bride of the Monster* DVD.

You can't just box up my life and give it away.

I blinked hard and stumbled into the backyard, slumping down on my old swing beside the sandbox Rajen and I had played in as little kids. A movement in the grass caught my eye. I looked up to see a pair of my father's old holey boxers crawling across the lawn.

"What in the . . ."

Had television finally killed off my brain cells, just like Mom warned? The underwear kept floating across the lawn, and I tiptoed over to find it clenched between the teeth of a gray and white kitten.

I picked her up. She fit into one of my hands, paws cold on my palm. I rubbed my cheek against her soft fur. She smelled like saltwater, seaweed, and tar.

"*Mew!*" she cried and reached to touch my face with white velvet paws.

Her ribs stuck out, and her sides looked hollow. She wasn't wearing a collar.

You're solitary, too.

I tucked her inside my sweatshirt and walked upstairs into my parents' bedroom. They stood in front of two suitcases. Voluntary Simplicity meant they could take only the clothes that would fit. Beside my father's already-crammed case sat a pile of suits and ties. Mom held a Saks dress she couldn't squash into her packed suitcase. "I could wear it on the drive to Oregon." She smoothed it into a rectangle and dropped it on the bed. "But . . ." she sighed, "I don't *need* it."

"I need this kitten."

The words surprised all of us. On cue, the kitten stuck her head out of my sweatshirt and mewed. "This is not a super . . . superflu . . . super-whatever frivolity," I said. "It's a *need*."

My words shocked all of us. I'd never been a cat person. Or a dog person. Especially not a bird person, thanks to Hitchcock's eye-gouging crows. I liked Rajen's mice just fine, but Blinky took care of them whenever Rajen's family visited his grandparents in Pakistan. Still, everything inside me cried out to keep this kitten, like if I could just hold onto its little purring body, my life wouldn't spin out of control.

As if it agreed, the kitten mewed again, all pink tongue and white needle teeth.

"Oh . . . dear." Mom couldn't help herself. She stretched out a finger and stroked the kitten's fuzzy gray head. We looked toward my father for his approval.

But Dad was just standing there staring down at a red necktie, winding it around and around his wrist. I looked away.

"Your kitty will have a whole acre to play on in Oregon!" Mom said too loudly, making the decision herself. "She's adorable."

I carried the kitten to my room and set her on the bed in a pile of laundry. She rubbed her cheek hard against my hand, then gnawed on one of my socks, purring like crazy.

"Are you real?" I scratched under her white chin, and she erupted into hard-core purring.

If she *was* real, then so was the move to Oregon.

•

My father built a cage for the kitten out of a wooden orange crate and some wire. On the morning of our epic move, he wedged the contraption behind my seat in the purple Volkswagen bus Mom had bought to replace her Corvette. I coaxed the kitten into the carrier with some Friskies and latched the door.

"Well, this is it!" Dad thumped the SOLD sign with his fist and grabbed my mother's hands. "Say good-bye to Hollywood!" he sang, swinging her in a circle.

"And good riddance!" she laughed.

Anger burned in my gut. How could they be so happy when they'd ruined my life?

My father climbed into the moving van and waved. He looked small and vulnerable in the high seat. But his lips stretched in a huge, manic smile. I ducked my head and shoved my skateboard into the bus.

This is all your fault, Dad.

But if I got really honest with myself, shoved the anger aside, I knew deep down that we had to move. We couldn't stay in this house, in this life. Not after what had happened.

For weeks, I'd tried to shove the memory away. But now it flashed through my head like a scene from an old horror movie you can't help watching over and over even though it scares the pants off you. This is how I wrote it the night that it happened, but I never showed it to anyone, not even to Mr. Davies.

FADE IN
EXTERIOR. FRIDAY IN MAY - REDONDO BEACH
- EVENING.

MOM walks over to meet SOLO at the library.
He says good-bye to his two friends. He
and his mother talk and laugh, and stop
on the way home for Japanese takeout.
Solo swings the bag full of cartons of
rice and vegetables. He inhales the steam
wafting up from the bag and smiles.

CLOSE-UP of elegant two-story house with
the ocean in the background. PAN IN on
the garage. Exhaust fumes seep from a
crack in the closed door.

                    MOM
    Is that *smoke* coming from the garage?

She drops her purse and races into the
house. Solo stands on the lawn. He looks
confused. He's still clutching the bag of
food. In a moment, the automatic garage
door rolls up to reveal a red Corvette in
a haze of bluish exhaust. A black Shop-
Vac tube stretches from the tailpipe to
the driver's side window.

MOM (CONT'D)
Call 9-1-1! *Now*, Solo!

She yanks open the car door. Big band music—the kind from old black and white movies—fills the garage.

Cartons spill rice and vegetables onto the sidewalk. Solo overturns his mother's purse. Not seeing a cell phone, he races into the house.

INTERIOR. LIVING ROOM WITH WHITE CARPET AND TALL BOOKCASES

CLOSE-UP on Solo's hands—they shake as he snatches the cell phone from the table and punches in numbers and an EMT answers.

SOLO
(into phone)
There's an emergency!

DISPATCHER
State location and nature of problem, please.

SAY GOOD-BYE TO HOLLYWOOD

> SOLO
>
> I'm at my house! I don't know what the problem is. I think our garage is on fire!

Solo shouts out his address, then hangs up the phone and yells up the stairs.

> SOLO (CONT'D)
>
> Dad? You up there? I think the Corvette just exploded!

No answer. Solo stands in the living room, staring out the window at smoke filling the air. Neighbors begin to appear in their front yards. They point toward the garage, horror evident on their faces.

LONG SHOT through window. A fire engine and an ambulance speed screaming up the street. Solo's eyes widen, and his mouth gapes with horror as three paramedics carry a limp, lifeless Japanese man out of the garage on a stretcher. Behind them, Solo's mother, sobbing.

> SOLO (CONT'D)
>
> Dad? *Dad!*

FADE OUT

"Solo? Dude, are you alive?" Rajen stood in front of me, surfboard under one arm. He waved his hand in front of my eyes. Blinky hovered beside him, his wet suit pulled down around his waist. I leaped in front of the purple bus like I could hide it with my body.

"What's up, bros?" I managed to squeak.

We stood there feeling stupid because only two of us had on wet suits, and one of us was smuggling his inside a pillowcase so his mom wouldn't sell it.

I rubbed my eyes. "Sand," I muttered.

Blinky just gazed at me through his thick glasses, silent. But Rajen gave me a back-slapping hug and dropped something into my hand. "Open it when you get to Oregon."

I looked down at an Altoids tin. "Uh . . . thanks." I dropped it into my backpack.

Rajen glanced at my parents and lowered his voice. "I'm getting the tree house ready. I'll email you tonight. We need a code so we can plot your escape. We'll call it . . . Operation Surf's Up."

"We won't have a computer for a few days," I mumbled, leaving out the part about how Voluntary Simplicity meant no computer, *ever*, and no cell phone for me until college.

"Then I'll send you postcards. Stay cool, okay?"

I chewed my thumbnail. "Yep."

My friends headed down to the beach. They'd surf all morning, come back to chow hot dogs wrapped in naan bread at Rajen's, then head out again. By the time they came in for the night—their hair stiff with salt and their arm muscles aching—I'd be in Oregon. No ocean, no friends, nothing but a gray and white kitten with an appetite for old boxer shorts.

Mom started up the Volkswagen. It coughed and sputtered black smoke. I slumped down in the seat so no neighbors could see me. Dad saluted us from the U-Haul. We pulled away from our house—from my room with the glow-in-the-dark stars on the ceiling and the back-yard where I'd had birthday parties for thirteen years.

I watched through the back window as the wide line of ocean grew smaller and smaller. The lump in my throat swelled bigger and bigger until I thought I'd throw up.

But there was my kitten, climbing over the seats with a pair of Mom's flowered socks in her mouth, landing on Mom's shoulder with her claws extended.

"Ow!" Mom laughed. "Your father's never been very good at carpentry. Must not have latched the door on that cage." She let the kitten ride on her shoulder and play with her braids.

"You look like an Indian," I said, plucking the kitten off her tie-dyed shirt and cuddling her to my chest.

My mother hugged the giant steering wheel. "I feel like Sacagawea, headed for the unknown. Think of the screenplays you'll write, Solo. We're going to have a wonderful time!"

I buried my face in the kitten's fur. She put her paws on my eyes, then licked off the saltwater. It would be hard to run away with a kitten.

We'll have to cross rivers and mountains, and when we get back to California, Steven Spielberg will make a movie about us.

"You'll have so many adventures," my mother kept talking. "You can hunt for blackberries and build forts in the forest around our house. At night, we'll sit on the porch and learn the names of the stars. We can buy a telescope with the yard sale money. . . ."

Mom's idea of fun sounded ridiculous. Running away would be the real adventure.

"What's your kitty's name, Solo?" She reached over to rub the back of my neck.

I squirmed away. "I dunno."

Like I said before, labels are important. I was still working to come up with a good one for the kitten. But she never had a name, because a week after we moved to Oregon, she escaped through a hole in the trailer's screen door and was murdered.

Chapter Four

THE STRONGEST STORIES
ARE BORN OF PAIN

Saturday morning, after my first week of forced labor at the raptor center, I woke up to the sound of waves breaking.

Maybe it was all a nightmare. Maybe I'm still in California and I can go surfing.

I jumped out of bed to find pine trees rustling in the breeze outside the trailer window.

My heart hurt.

Seven a.m. Fourteen hours until I could go back to sleep. My skateboard stood abandoned in my closet. No way could I do grabs and pipes on the long potholed driveway that led to our house.

No computer or TV meant no emailing Rajen and Blinky and no movies. I couldn't go hiking in the woods—who knew what terror lurked out there. I glanced at the boxer shorts on my bedpost and my throat tightened. No kitten to play with, either.

Finally, I pulled out the book Minerva had dropped onto my backpack. *One Man's Owl.* Apparently, the author had raised an orphaned baby owl and eventually turned it loose in the forest. Big deal. Two months ago, you couldn't have paid me to read that book.

Now, there was nothing else to do.

My mother walked in as I finished the second chapter. "Solo, Eric's mother called. She invited you to go fishing."

A single sunbeam streamed through the window and lit up my mother's face, illuminating the wrinkles around her eyes. I closed the book and shoved it under my pillow.

"No, Mom, I hate fishing. I'd rather just . . ." I almost said "read," but then I remembered *what* I was reading. If she saw the book, Mom would think I was turning into Enraged Kitten Avenger again. I'd be back in juvenile corrections before you could say "dead mice for breakfast."

"I'd rather just hang out here."

Mom pursed her lips. She looked almost normal today in her white Versace dress, but something flashed on one bare foot. A silver toe ring. I snorted, and she moved her foot a little behind the other. "I've got an interview at the university, and your father's taking the bus to see his psychologist, then to the library to do some research. You can't stay home alone."

"But you let me stay home in Redondo Beach all the time!"

"Well . . . things are different in Oregon." Her eyes flickered away from mine.

I'm different. File "Solo" under At-Risk Youth.

I pulled the covers over my head, hoping she'd take the hint and leave. Instead, her bare feet grew roots, and she turned up the volume. "Eric's father is away on business. His mother offered to drive you and Eric down to the canal, then take you out to lunch. I want you to go."

"Why?" I hurled my pillow across the room. My mother's mouth opened, but nothing came out. "You want me to catch a *fish*? I thought we were vegetarians!"

She picked up the pillow and gave it a few good whacks. "We're pescatarians—vegetarians who eat fish. Salmon twice a week's good for your father's recovery." She stopped beating up my pillow and hugged it to her chest. "When I was your age, my sisters and I wandered all over these woods having a marvelous time. Sometimes I wish you weren't an only child." She addressed the pillow. "That was a mistake."

"Yeah, one of many."

Mom shot me a warning look, but forced a glorious white smile. "Isn't it wonderful that you and Eric live next door to each other, and you're only a year apart? You'll be best friends."

I thought of Rajen. By now, we'd be out shredding waves while my mom and her friends did the same thing a little ways down the beach. Later, she'd shower and drink espresso on the Starbucks patio—all the stuff she used to do on Saturdays before she turned into an alien.

"Eric's not my friend," I reasoned. "I can't believe his mom even wants me around him. His dad said I can't go near him, remember?"

"Let's not get into that again."

Mom sat on the edge of the bed and searched the room. It was pretty clean, for me. My old room had been huge. You couldn't see the carpet underneath all my clothes and magazines. But I could walk across this trailer bedroom in five steps. I'd taped surfing posters over the nail holes in the walls and stacked my screen-play notebooks on top of the mouse-chewed carpet in one corner. No superfluous frivolities here, unless you counted Mom's old Darth Vader bank on my dresser. When you dropped in a coin, it did that deep breathing thing and James Earl Jones's voice garbled something about the dark side.

"This bank was mine when I was your age," she'd told me the day we moved to Oregon and she unpacked the boxes.

I took it, not to make her happy, but because strangers had bought up all my DVDs and stuff at the yard sale. Now I had a bank full of quarters and dimes. But my life was empty.

As soon as Darth's filled, I'm getting out of here.

My mother stood up. "Kitchen, ten minutes. Your father's making waffles." She walked out.

"This is so stupid!" I yanked on a T-shirt and shorts and wedged a pencil and notebook into my back pocket. It used to take me half an hour to make my bed. My kitten loved to attack the sheets. We'd have wild games of Chase Solo's Fingers until she collapsed on my pillow. Then, I'd brush her until she stretched out long and purring.

Never again.

I stuffed Minerva's book far beneath the mattress. Between the pages, I saw the edge of a postcard. A picture of a bunch of stupid birds from the raptor center. I pulled it out.

It was blank, so I scribbled a note.

Hey Rajen,

Snore-egon sucks—nothing but trees and birds. Saving $ for Operation Surf's Up. Back soon.

Your friend,
Solo

I tucked the postcard into my newest screenplay notebook. Eric's mom was cool—I could persuade her to swing by the post office downtown, and she wouldn't ask questions.

The trailer kitchen was so small that barely one person could fit in it at a time. My father stood beside the stove all tied up in a red checked apron, pouring waffle batter into a hot iron. When I squished past him to the fridge, he leaned over and gave me a one-arm hug. "Good morning!"

"Not really." I poured orange juice and sat at the table with my back to him so I wouldn't have to look at his apron. In California, Dad had worn khakis and a leather bomber jacket. Now, he wandered around in cutoff blue jeans and a T-shirt with a big yellow happy face on the front. His hair hung shaggy over his ears. But I had to admit he made killer waffles. I never knew he could cook before.

"Tofu, sugarless jam, soy milk, tempeh . . ." I searched the fridge for maple syrup. "Mom expects us to *eat* this stuff?"

My mother walked out of the bathroom and reached into a cupboard. "Try these on your waffles." She handed me a jar of spiced apples. "They're healthier than syrup." She put a hand on my bandaged wrist for an instant, then turned away. "I'd better go. The bus needs time to get over the hill."

The Hill loomed long and steep on the road beyond our house, inevitable if you wanted to get downtown. My skateboard could make it to the top faster than The Big Grape.

Mom gave Dad a quick hug. "Are you feeling okay? Figured out the bus schedule?" Her eyes searched his, and her hands clutched his shoulder blades beneath his shirt.

Dad's hollow cheekbones lifted in a tight smile, giving his happy face T-shirt some fierce competition. "I'm great! Good luck with your interview."

Mom released him then, and her words flew out high and fast. "The university is full of fascinating history. I'd love to teach there. I'm off to yoga after the interview, okay? Have a good day, boys!"

My father's hundred-watt smile dimmed as she walked out of the trailer. "She really wants this job."

I shrugged and dumped spiced apples over my waffle. She'd had a good job in Redondo Beach. We both knew why she'd quit.

He stared out the window above the sink. Back home, we could watch waves crashing to shore while we washed dishes. But here, everything just blew around in the breeze, a billion shades of green—trees, bushes, grass. *Boring.*

My father cleared his throat. "I'm going to the library to research Japanese internment. Did you know your grandparents were forced to leave their home and relocate to a camp in California, because the government thought Japanese Americans were a threat during World War II?" His eyes glistened. "My father was a business owner, respected throughout his community."

I put down my fork. The hypocrisy was killing me. Here was Dad crying because someone made his parents leave their home for a year . . . but he'd made me leave my home forever.

"Dad, you've told me this story a million times," I sighed.

My father went back to gazing out the window while his waffle burned to a crisp, and I sat there biting my tongue so I wouldn't say anything else to upset him. I swear, I was almost glad when Mrs. Miller's green pickup rumbled into the driveway. Eric bounced on the front seat, rocking out to country music.

"There's my ride. Fishing date. Mom's orders."

I looked at Dad sideways to see if he'd spare the fish and spoil the child. But he didn't notice. "Catch a big one," he mumbled.

I reached into the fridge for my water bottle. My father stood so near I could see the corner of his eye twitching.

Up close, it was hard to hate him.

I followed his gaze to see what he was staring at. A fly, trying like crazy to escape a spiderweb stretched across one corner of the window. As I watched, the spider crept up and injected the fly with venom, then wrapped it up tight in a silk shroud. I bit my lip.

What if he's not here when I get back?

I pushed the thought away and walked out the door. But halfway down the driveway, I froze. Sweat jumped out all over my body. *Is this the first time he's been alone since he tried to . . .?*

I sprinted back into the kitchen to find Dad pulling a bottle of maple syrup from behind stacked cans of tomatoes and beans.

"Oops!" His face flushed like a kid who's been caught sneaking Oreos before dinner.

Relief turned to anger. I stomped down the hall and snatched up my Dodgers hat, then stalked back out the door without looking at my father. If he wanted to hoard secrets, that was his problem, but he could've let me in on his sugar stash.

"Howdy, Solo!" Mrs. Miller called to me in her Texas accent. She reached across her son and opened the pickup door. "Good to see you, honey."

Now, I felt like a pathetic little loser. I hadn't seen Eric or his mother since we'd sat in the courtroom and his father tried to throw me in jail. I messed around with the straps on my backpack so I wouldn't have to meet her eyes. "Hi, Mrs. M.," I mumbled. "Hey, Eric."

"Hi, Solo!" Eric smiled his humongous smile and scooted close to his mom, making room for me on the bench seat. A white bandage peeked through his brown hair, which was cut in an upside-down bowl shape like The Beatles had when they were really young—I saw their picture on the record album my dad had. The spiced apples squirmed in my stomach.

The Millers lived on the next acre over. Before my parents bought the trailer, Eric and his mother had hiked around on our land, picking blackberries and cutting back the poison oak. Mrs. Miller walked over the day we moved in, arms full of pies and canned fruit from her trees. My mother told her, "*Mi casa es su casa,*" which is Spanish for "My house is your house." That's when I met Eric. He thought my parents' pond was his pond.

Now, I wished I'd never found him crouched down in the mud beside the water with his stupid magnifying glass.

"I hear the fish are jumping in the canal." Mrs. Miller turned her truck toward the riverside park downtown. "If you boys catch some, we'll fry 'em up for dinner. I've got a hair appointment and I need to swing by the garden store, but I'll be back by noon. Then we can mosey on over to McMenamins for burgers and fries."

Eric clapped his hands. "We have ice cream?"

"You got it." Her cowboy hat bobbed up and down. "We'll rope ourselves a chocolate cone or two."

Ice cream.

Apparently, my mother hadn't told Mrs. Miller about the no sugar rule. I looked out the window at a flock of white geese strutting across the road and smiled grimly. What Mom didn't know wouldn't hurt her . . . or me.

Eric's mom let us out near the university's mammoth football stadium. "See y'all at noon." She leaned over to kiss her son's head. There was way too much kissing in Oregon. People here didn't shake hands or slap five. They smooched—heads, cheeks, lips. *Gross.*

I jumped out of the truck before Mrs. Miller could plant a wet one on me, but she got ahold of my arm. "Thank you, Solo. This is the first time Eric's ever had a playdate with a friend."

A *playdate*? If Rajen and Blinky were here, they'd crack up at the sight of me loaded down with fishing poles, running after some thick-tongued kid in a T-shirt silkscreened with beetles.

"C'mon, Solo!" Eric hollered, swinging his red plastic tackle box. "Let's rope us a salmon!"

There were other kids fishing at the canal. I pulled my hat brim low over my eyes. Someone snickered. Across the water, a boy pointed his fishing pole at me and laughed.

"Shark bait," I muttered. "Couldn't catch a wave if it rose up under your butt." Didn't he know fishing was for old men hunched over the pier? The *cool* kids surfed.

Eric sat cross-legged in a patch of dandelions with his fishing pole. He looked like a mushroom in his brown hat stuck through with feathered lures.

"Want a red one!" He chose a plastic worm from his tackle box. "Help me hook it, Solo?"

"Can't you do it?"

He shook his head. I smashed the fake worm onto his hook. He stood up and flung the pole back. I jumped out of the way as he flipped it over his head and cast his line far into the canal.

"Yikes, Eric. Watch it!"

"I fly fishing." His tongue stuck out between chapped lips as he yanked his pole out of the water and flung it back. Again, I heard snickering. I grabbed the other pole and collapsed on a nearby log.

I cast my line into the canal and watched the dogs running in the park across from me. The sun tried hard to burn a hole through my T-shirt. I reached into my backpack for sunscreen, and my fingers touched a cool rectangle. The Altoids tin Rajen had given me before I left California.

I wedged the fishing pole under the log and popped off the lid. *Sand.* Redondo Beach sand. I poured it into my hand. There were shells, too, and a piece of green glass the ocean had smoothed into a jewel. I sniffed. The sand smelled salty and sweet.

I swallowed hard and poured it back into the tin. My eyes stung. I pulled my baseball cap down, hiding my face from the kids across the canal.

"LA Dodgers are losers!" someone hollered. Someone else laughed.

Then I remembered something Mr. Davies once told our screenwriting class: *The strongest stories are born of pain.*

I reached into my pocket for my notebook and pencil.

FADE IN
EXTERIOR. CROWDED BEACH – DAY

GUYS and GIRLS with surfboards stand on the sand, looking out to sea. They're pointing and shrieking. The camera follows one girl's finger across the water

to where SOLO HAHN rides the crest of a
twenty-foot wave.

                    GIRL #1
It's Solo Hahn. Look at him go!

                    GIRL #2
I heard that he loved the ocean so
much he ran away from his parents at
only thirteen. He lived in a tree
house and surfed ten hours a day,
since he couldn't go to school. Now,
there's no wave he can't ride.

The crowd goes wild, cheering for the
champion surfer. Solo raises one hand to
wave, and then . . .

"Why d'you hang out with retards?"
I looked up from my notebook and blinked at a
skinny kid with shoulder-length wavy hair—so blond
it was white—and a missing front tooth. He sneered at
me, hands stuffed into baggy shorts pockets.
"This my friend Solo!" Eric tottered over to us. "He
live in a trailer next door."
Missing Tooth loved that. "Hiya, trailer trash."
There was another kid—even shorter than me,
with curly hair flattened under a bandana and a blue

fisherman's hat. He scrunched up his sunburned nose. "My dad's a cop at juvenile court. He said you shot the retard with his father's gun. You gotta play with him, or you'll go to jail, right?"

"He's not a retard." I glanced at Eric's beetle T-shirt. "He's got Down syndrome, that's all."

"Whatever." Missing Tooth stared at the bandage around my wrist. "So what about that gun?"

I covered my wrist with my hand. "None of your business."

Three weeks in Oregon and I already had a reputation. Forget new kid on the block—I was the new gangster on the block.

"Solo! Help me!" Eric pointed to his fishing hook, wedged high into a tree branch. "It stuck!"

The two boys practically fell on the ground laughing. I prayed for one of Ed Wood's B-movie spaceships to drop down and whisk them away to some Styrofoam-planet galaxy a billion light years away. "Stop fly fishing!" I scowled at Eric and hauled myself into the tree. "Just drop your hook in the water and leave it, okay, Eric?"

"Okay, Solo."

By the time I got the hook unstuck, Missing Tooth and his friend were gone. Eric grinned. "You the best!" His face glowed pink and sweaty. He rubbed it with one arm, and his bandage fluttered to the ground. I could see a long, crusted-over scab above his right eye.

"Ow. I cut my leg on that tree." I rubbed my ankle and looked across the river. Missing Tooth ran over a bridge with his short friend. They met another kid with a dog on a leash and took off toward the woods.

I reached into my pocket and touched the tin full of sand. Rajen and Blinky and I were supposed to go to high school together in a year—the Three Musketeers, only cooler. Now I was just cold—lonely as a glacier.

All that afternoon, I couldn't stop thinking about the question Missing Tooth had asked me. Even when Mrs. Miller handed Eric and me each a double scoop of chocolate raspberry truffle from the shop near the university, the white-haired kid's words wouldn't stop echoing in my head.

What about that gun?

Shooting it was the worst decision I'd ever made in my life.

CHAPTER FIVE
MENACE TO SOCIETY

I might've gone my whole life without firing a gun if I hadn't met Eric. He was my age, but he acted like a little kid. A week after my parents dragged me to Oregon, he bounced into my life like one of those grasshoppers he was so gung ho about. I'd been holed up in the trailer with a stack of surfing magazines when my kitten padded through the door with Mom's ponytail holder in her teeth. She dropped it at my feet.

"What'cha want, kitty cat?" I looked up from an ad for Costa Rica and some of the best surfing in the world.

She mewed, eyes on the red circle of elastic. I tossed it across the room. She raced after it, pounced, and carried it back to me.

"You can fetch?"

We played for an hour—me throwing, her retrieving, until she collapsed purring on my pillow. That's when I got the stupidest idea I'd ever had—I decided to find her a lizard to play with. I didn't have anything against reptiles. I was just bored.

"I'll be back." I kissed the top of her soft head. She reached out one white paw and yawned like she was saying good-bye.

Outside, rain clouds hung heavy and gray. Frog—not lizard—weather. I trudged through the trees toward the pond. If Rajen and Blinky were here, we could build forts and race model boats, but there was no point in doing that stuff alone.

Suddenly, a grasshopper jumped across my path and a weird-looking kid leaped out from behind a tree. He peered at me through a big black-handled magnifying glass hung on a string around his neck.

"What are *you* looking at?" I stared back at him.

"Dragonfly!" He pointed to a shimmering blue insect above my head.

The kid looked stocky, short arms and legs and a football player's thick neck. His eyelids slanted a little, like mine.

"I Eric Miller." He pronounced his *R*s like *W*s. "What your name?"

"Uh . . . Solo Hahn."

He flashed a wide, crazy smile. I edged away from him, but he wasn't finished with me. "You like Han Solo from *Star Wars*?"

Surprised, I answered, "Yeah. My mom's nuts about that movie."

Eric stepped out of the tall grass, knees muddy and grass stained under his denim shorts. "Wanna see my house? I have cookies."

I couldn't help it—I felt sorry for the guy. Here he was all alone in the woods on a summer day, nothing to do but stalk dragonflies. He probably didn't have a single friend. Never in a million years would I have hung out with Eric in California, but I thought Rajen would probably forgive me this once. I mean, the guy had cookies and I was craving sugar.

I looked through the trees toward the trailer. Mom had gone to the market. Dad was hunched over an ancient typewriter in his bedroom, banging out research notes for his novel. A sign hanging from his doorknob read: GENIUS AT WORK—DON'T DISTURB.

"Where do you live?" I spoke slowly, so Eric could understand me. Turned out I was the slow one.

"I live next door to you!"

Only one house stood close to the trailer—a two-story with a red roof just visible through the trees. "Well . . . I guess I'll come over. But just for a minute," I said.

I followed Eric down a dirt path. Blackberry branches snagged my legs, gouging skinny trails of blood. Eric dodged the brambles with surprising grace and kept up a running commentary about bugs.

"Gnat!" We stepped through a cloud of little winged things, and I almost died coughing. "Yellow jacket! Cicada!" We stopped in front of his house. "Shoofly." He pointed to a green-winged fly on the door.

I had to laugh. "That's just a fly."

"Nope. *Shoofly*. Come in."

I could tell Eric's mother didn't follow my mom's no sugar rule. A big, duck-shaped cookie jar practically quacked on the kitchen table. Eric grabbed two mammoth chocolate chip cookies and gave me one.

For an instant, I felt almost happy. Eric's house reminded me of our place in Redondo Beach—white carpet, huge leather couch. Bookcases towered everywhere. I studied one shelf. *Count Us In: Growing Up with Down Syndrome. A Parent's Guide to Down Syndrome. The Upside of Down.*

I knew Down syndrome was some kind of disability you were born with. My old school had a special class for kids like Eric. They ate lunch by themselves in the cafeteria and didn't go to surf club or screenwriting class. If I passed them in the hall, they said hi and I said hi back—but I never invited them to my house or to a bonfire on the beach.

Why didn't I?

Eric grabbed my hand. "Come see my room!"

"Okay . . . but just for a sec. Then I hafta go feed my kitten."

Eric's bedroom could've doubled as a science lab. Bug posters covered the walls. Jars full of plants and mysterious sludge crammed the windowsills. A microscope and two aquariums sat on the dresser.

"Look, Solo. Walking sticks!"

The walking sticks in the aquarium looked like twigs. How cool would that be, to walk up wooden window sills completely camouflaged? You could listen to people's conversations undercover. Maybe then, you'd understand why they did the things they did.

I thought of my father alone in the trailer. *There are knives in the kitchen. A rope clothesline. The propane stove. What if he tries to kill himself again?*

"I better go."

A shaggy black dog burst into the room and jumped up on Eric, mammoth paws on his shoulders. "Down, Hank!" Eric hollered.

The dog returned to all fours. He lumbered over and shoved his wet nose into my hand, tail wagging. I scratched behind his fuzzy ears. "Dude. He's as big as a pony."

"Howdy!" A tall woman in a cowboy hat appeared. "What'cha doing, partners?"

Eric threw his arm across my shoulders. "This my friend, Mom. His name Han Solo!"

I tensed. Back home, boys didn't touch other boys except to slap each other five after a killer wave. But Eric was different—he didn't know any better. I let the arm stay.

"My name's Solo Hahn."

Mrs. Miller didn't make the usual jokes like, "Where's Chewbacca?" or "Watch out for Darth Vader." She just shook my hand. "Pleased to meet you, honey. Eric's daddy's working late tonight, so we have extra pork chops and a big ol' chocolate cake. How 'bout I call your mama and tell her you're staying for supper?"

It was the chocolate cake that got me. *Stupid*. If I could've rewritten the scene, I would have told Mrs. Miller thanks, but no thanks. Because if I hadn't stayed for dinner, Eric and I wouldn't have unlocked the door to his father's off-limits office and swiped an encyclopedia while his mom was in the kitchen making corn bread. I wouldn't have spotted the shotgun hanging high above his dad's desk. And I would've been home in time to rescue my kitten, who chewed off the tape my father had stapled over the hole in the rusting screen door.

But I did stay for dinner, and I was too late.

After dessert, Mrs. Miller left Eric watching *Bill Nye the Science Guy* and his lecture on insects while she drove me home. "Too dark to walk through the forest, honey. All sorts of wild animals out there."

I blinked at her. "Like what?"

"Well, mostly just raccoons." She chuckled. "But they get mean if you surprise 'em."

"Just let me out by the mailbox." The trailer looked even trashier in the dark, a giant can of Spam tossed into the field after a picnic.

"All righty." She put a foil-wrapped piece of chocolate cake into my hands. "I'm running down to the market for some milk. Eric's daddy'll be home in half an hour. The man can't eat cake without a glass of milk."

I got out of the truck. "Thanks for dinner, Mrs. M. It was really good . . . especially dessert."

She smiled. "You're a sweet boy. Come over and play with Eric anytime. He could use a friend."

I mumbled something and closed the door, thinking of how to hide the piece of cake from my parents.

As I walked up the dark driveway, big band music poured out of the trailer's open windows. My parents were slow dancing in the living room—Mom had her head thrown back, laughing in the candlelight. The sky glowed navy over the treetops.

Suddenly, something flapped over my head. A swift sweep of wind ruffled my hair, and a tiny cry sounded behind me. I turned and dropped my cake.

Mew! I heard, and then the scream that would stay with me forever.

Meowwwwwww!

"Oh no . . . *no!*"

I leapt off the porch and ran toward the sound.

But the owl had gotten there before me.

I lunged toward it. The owl tumbled into a bush and flapped its wings, trying to free itself. I grabbed at it and talons seized my right wrist. Dug in. Punctured flesh.

My left hand flailed. A beak jabbed into my arm. Yellow eyes flooded mine. I yelped in pain.

The owl let go of my wrist. Lifted, wings wide, and merged with the darkness. My kitten dangled from its talons.

"*No!*"

The murderer sailed over my head. I crashed down the path after it, wrist throbbing.

Branches ripped at my arms and legs. "Come back!"

The creature glided up through the trees and vanished.

I fell to the ground, clutching my bloody arm. "No! Please, no!"

Nature was a horrible thing. It snatched up anything weak and helpless and slaughtered it.

"She was so little," I cried. "I promised to protect her."

Maybe there was still time.

If I could get to the owl, stop it somehow. . . .

An image flashed into my head.

The shotgun.

I jumped up and raced through the stabbing blackberry vines toward Eric's house. Hank jumped up barking as I burst through the door. Eric sat cross-legged on the couch, watching TV in his pajamas. "Solo? Your arm bleeding!"

"I need to borrow your dad's shotgun!"

He shook his head. "Unh-uhn. That gun off-limits. My father say so." He peered at me through his magnifying glass. "Why your eyes wet?"

She was so small. I could still feel her paws against my cheek.

I smothered a sob. "I need that gun! Something . . . someone took something."

Eric's forehead wrinkled. "Oh, you shoot a robber?" he said slowly. "My father say that okay."

For the second time that night, he reached into a tobacco pouch on the bookshelf and fished out a key. Then he ran to unlock his dad's office door. He hoisted a chair onto the desk, climbed up, and reached for the gun. "Here you go."

I'd never held a gun. It was heavier than I'd expected. In movies, people made it look so easy—they just held out their weapon and fired it. I wasn't sure I could even lift the thing high enough to aim for the owl. I slung it over my shoulder and stumbled outside.

Now the moon was up, a huge yellow disk. It lit the path to the pond, but tears filled my eyes. I tripped on a rock and almost dropped the gun.

"Watch out!" Eric cried.

I spun around. "What're you doing here? Go home!"

"I come with you. Kick some robbers."

That was my second mistake—letting Eric come with me. But how could I tell him no? It was his father's gun, after all.

We crawled under the barbed-wire fence and stopped to listen. Nothing but the chirp of cicadas, and then *WHOO-hoo-oo-oo-oo-WHOO-WHOO!*

Something rustled in the trees.

"Great horned owl," Eric whispered.

Maybe my kitten was still alive. I gripped the cold metal and cocked back the trigger, the way I'd seen people do in movies. Suddenly, the owl glided across a clearing, flapping its huge wings. Talons gripped a fuzzy gray and white body. I still had time to save her.

I pulled the trigger right as Eric darted in front of me. "No, Solo!"

The gun barrel struck my shoulder. Eric fell to the ground.

The world went silent.

Eric curled into a ball and held his eye with both hands. Blood seeped out between his fingers. "Ouch," he mouthed.

"Oh . . . *crap.*" My knees buckled and I slid to the ground. *What if I've blown his eye off?*

I hugged my knees to my chest, shaking.

What do I do?

I closed my eyes and rocked back and forth in the dark, gasping for breath in the swampy night air. Mosquitoes rose off the pond and spun around us, stinging welts into my arms and legs.

Should I carry Eric back to his house? Take him to my parents? Should I run away? What should I do?

Eric's father didn't let me wonder for long.

Hank led him straight to us. The man's eyes went from the gun on the ground to his son's bloody face. His black trench coat swirled around him as he bent to pick up Eric. He stalked off into the trees without looking at me.

Who knows how long I sat there, tears and snot congealing on my chin. Over and over, I felt the owl's talons pierce my wrist. Again, I heard the scream, the tiny cry.

Suddenly, an arm yanked me to my feet. Sounds began to return, slamming against my eardrums. "Get up!"

Mr. Miller marched me through the forest to the trailer. My parents were still dancing in the living room. He pounded on the screen door.

"Didn't you hear the gunshot?" he demanded when they opened the door.

The happy notes of big band music surrounded us. My father's face went white at the sight of his son's arm covered in blood. My mother dug her nails into her palms.

"*What gunshot?*" they said in unison.

•

Eric ended up in the hospital with five stitches above his eye where the shot had grazed him. I ended up with eight weeks hard labor at the Raptor Rescue Center and a new label—At-Risk Youth.

FADE IN
INTERIOR. JUVENILE COURT - DAY

A judge sits at a high desk. Two tables below. At one sits ERIC MILLER, a kid with a football player's thick neck. He wore a bandage over one eye and a beetle T-shirt. MRS. MILLER sits on one side of him, her cowboy hat on the table. MR.

MILLER stands on the other in his trench coat. At the second table, MR. and MRS. HAHN sit near their son, SOLO. In their stylish clothes, they look like a magazine ad for a perfect family . . . except for their grim faces.

> MR. MILLER
> (pointing at Solo)
> That boy is a menace to society.
> Mr. Hahn chews his knuckles and looks sadly at Solo. But Mrs. Hahn leaps up, tears streaming down her cheeks.

> MRS. HAHN
> He's a straight-A student. He loved that kitten!

Mrs. Miller gives her a sympathetic look and addresses the judge in a Texas twang.

> MRS. MILLER
> It's our fault. I've told Paul a hundred times to lock up that shotgun.

The judge peers down at Solo and frowns. He brandishes his gavel.

                    JUDGE
Eight weeks of community service.
You're getting off easy this time.
Next time, you won't be so lucky.

Solo shuffles out of the courtroom, his
head hanging low. Mr. Miller leans over
as he passes behind Solo's parents; he
whispers something in Solo's ear.

                 MR. MILLER
                 (whispering)
You're a criminal. You should
be locked up.

FADE OUT

 That day in court, I knew my parents had chosen the
wrong name for me. I was about as far from a hero as
you could get. Mom should've named me Darth Vader,
Lord of the Dark Side, instead.
 Now, here in Oregon, kids I didn't even know had
slapped a new label on me.
 I was the scary kid . . . *the bad kid.*

Chapter Six

SERGEANT BIRD NERD

This bus is a piece of cr . . . *poop!*"

"Poop?"

A laugh rose in my throat, bitter as acid. My arms and back muscles hurt from loading bags of trout into the raptor center's deep freezer for the eagles. The last thing I wanted to do was go hiking. But when Mom picked me up after my second week of community service, The Big Grape made it to the bottom of that giant hill on the road to the trailer, then hacked a miserable hiccup and seized.

My mother's lips shaped curses, but she'd given up swearing along with sugar.

"The Corvette never even had a flat tire." I opened the door and felt a blast of hot air. "It was an awesome ride."

Mom heaved a bag of groceries into her arms and slammed her door shut with her butt. "I don't want to hear it, Solo. It won't kill us to walk a mile."

I jumped ship, and she handed me a bag from the backseat. My arm muscles groaned in protest. I plodded behind her at the side of the road, sweating waterfalls down my shirt. Mom's sandals slapped the ground, smashing little waffle imprints into the dirt.

Just make it to the mailbox.

I pictured Rajen's postcard waiting for me. I hadn't heard from him in a couple of weeks; I wondered if he'd gotten my card or if one of his nosy sisters intercepted it. The bag in my arms held all the refrigerator groceries; I felt the paper dampen and rip under my hot hands. "I'm gonna lose the tofu," I told Mom.

"Just hold on, Solo. We're almost there."

We made it to the two dented silver boxes nailed to a crooked wooden shelf. Mrs. Miller and Eric met us there, down from their house to get their mail. Eric studied my sweaty face through his magnifying glass. "You go jogging?"

His mom looked up from a stack of letters. "Pretty hot for a . . . oh, what happened?"

Mom sighed. "The VW broke down."

"Oh, honey, I'm so sorry." Mrs. Miller reached for the bag of groceries in Mom's arms. "Eric, honey, take Solo's bag. He looks exhausted."

They walked us down to the trailer. I hated the thought of Mrs. Miller seeing my parents' metal shack, but she appeared not to notice the dented sides, the faded paint, or the torn screen door. "Solo, honey," she said, "you wanna come with us to the ballgame this weekend? Eric loves those Emeralds."

"Dodgers rule." The words flew out before I could stop myself.

Mom shot me the evil eye. I could practically see the lecture hovering in the air.

Mrs. Miller invites you to a ballgame after you shoot her son, and you give her cr . . . poop about it?

"Thanks for the invite, Mrs. M.," I mumbled to my sports sandals.

Eric slapped me five. "We catch a shoofly, Solo!"

Mrs. Miller grinned. "He means a fly ball." She and Eric held our grocery bags until Mom pushed through the front door. I took mine and the bottom gave way. My knee saved most of the groceries, but the tofu plopped to the ground.

"No harm done. I hear it makes real good cheese-cake." Mrs. Miller handed the package to Mom and registered the look on her face. "Well, we'll let you two go get cleaned up. See ya later."

"That woman is entirely too cheerful," Mom muttered. Like she always did now, she stood still in the doorway for a minute and listened. Probably took a big sniff, too, praying she wouldn't smell car exhaust. But we didn't have a garage anymore, and the only vehicle we owned was gathering moss a mile away.

"Michael!" Mom hollered. "Can you help us with the groceries?"

Dad appeared in the hallway. He just watched as we heaved the shredded bags up to the counter. "What happened?"

"What happened is the man who sold us the VW is a liar and a crook." Mom grabbed a green apple from the fruit bowl and chomped a vicious bite. Her face soured. "Looks like we'll be riding the city bus for a while."

I unloaded groceries into the fridge. Dad sat at the table where he'd apparently been shelling peas. He tore open a pod and popped a row of peas into a bowl with his thumb. "The city bus, huh? Public transportation seems like a reasonable aspect of Voluntary Simplicity."

"Easy for you to say." Mom glared at him. "You don't have to leave the house."

I shot her a shocked look. We weren't a yelling family. My parents never fought, not even after Dad tried to leave us.

But now, my mother closed her mouth in a hard, tight line and began to shell peas like her whole life depended on it.

My father shrugged, turned to me. "How's the screenwriter? Busy examining your existential angst?"

"Uh . . . I guess."

Did everyone's dad talk this way or only the ones who were writing a book? "You . . . you wanna read one of my screenplays?"

"Put it on top of my to-do pile in my office."

I didn't tell Dad I had thirty notebooks filled cover-to-cover with screenplay scenes. "Mr. Davies—he was my teacher, remember—he said I'm pretty good. I haven't written a whole one yet . . . I'm still looking for material. But if you're too busy . . ."

Dad's head lowered over the bowl of peas. "I'm taking a break from my novel. Writer's block."

My mother stopped shelling and scowled at me. I scowled back. In a movie, the audience would see that we were both freaking out about the same thing.

Is he suicidal again?

I went to the sink and ran hot water over my hands, scrubbing hard to get rid of the death smell. I'd fixed meals for forty-two birds that morning—mice and fish and even a whole chicken for the red-tailed hawks to share—Minerva's orders. Now I was glad my parents didn't cook meat. All that carnage would turn anyone vegetarian.

"By the way," I muttered, "the bus doesn't go to the raptor center. It stops a mile before."

Mom heaved another huge sigh. "Well, you'll just have to walk until the VW's fixed."

"But it's a hundred degrees outside!"

"Well, I'm sorry, Solo, but I just don't know what else . . ."

I turned and stalked down the hall. Halfway to my room, rage exploded inside me like a shook-up Coke. "I told you we should've kept the Corvette!"

I slammed my door so hard the trailer trembled.

•

The next morning, Dad's writer's block must've un-clogged. In his room, he hunched over his typewriter, pounding the keys. They exploded like gunfire.

"Normal writers use a computer," I muttered and walked to the kitchen for a banana and a bagel.

From the living room, Mom looked at me upside down, twisted into a yoga pose. "Have a good day, sweetheart."

"Yeah, right."

Already, the sun beat down on the gravel drive-way. I pushed my sunglasses onto my face and rode my skateboard on the narrow shoulder to the bus stop. One other person waited on the bench—an elderly woman with bright purple hair that matched her sneakers. I tried to picture my grandmother digging in her Beverly Hills garden with her straw hat tied over purple curls. Impossible.

The bus pulled up, and I headed for the back so I could keep an eye on Granny, plus a girl with pink braids and a man with a Mohawk striped black and white like a skunk.

I leaned toward Mr. Mohawk. "Know where I could find a computer? I've gotta email someone."

He squinted, and his eyebrow ring caught the light. "Try the library, man."

"Thanks."

"No problemo."

The bus let me off at the bottom of the steep road to the raptor center. I tried to ride my skateboard up the last mile, but it ended up riding me. I hauled it under my arm, quads and hamstrings shrieking.

"Ha ha ha ha!" Edgar laughed from her enclosure.

"What's so funny?" I stomped past the crow and dropped my skateboard on the lawn.

"You're late." A guy with a curly blond ponytail marched toward me, armed with a bucket and hose. "I'm Lucas. I work with at-risk kids at the center."

So this guy knew I was a criminal, too.

Lucas didn't look like a typical jail warden. He was maybe twenty-five. Torn jeans, stained with bleach. Green bandana on his head and a silver feather on a black beaded necklace. His nose curved like a hawk's beak. One long eyebrow stretched over it. A hawk tattoo rode his bicep. A real weirdo.

He looks like he's part bird.

Hermes hooted from the office. *WHOO-hoo-oo-oo-oo-WHOO-WHOO!*

The hair on the back of my neck stood up. Lucas called back—a perfect imitation: *WHOO-hoo-oo-oo-oo-WHOO-WHOO!*

The injured great horned owl in the treatment room added his two cents. The three of them were a regular feathered choir.

"Get some rubber gloves," Lucas ordered. "You don't want to clean enclosures with your bare hands." He jerked his chin toward the office. "They're in there."

"Can you . . . can you put that owl in its mew first?"

Lucas's eyebrow shot up, but he stepped through the screen door, pulled on a leather glove, and guided Hermes into the mew. I edged in behind him and grabbed the box of rubber gloves.

"We'll start with the spotted owls." Lucas talked fast. I had to listen hard to catch his words before they flew away. "Watch me from outside the enclosure, and then you can help with the falcons. *Always* keep enclosure doors locked." He waved the key attached to a wooden eagle head the size of my fist. "Never leave this in a padlock. Minerva's number-one rule."

I rolled my eyes. Locked doors were nothing new. After my father tried to kill himself, Mom locked the garage door and threw away the key.

I followed Lucas to a tall wood and wire enclosure. He unlocked the door, pulled in a hose and bucket, and latched the door behind him. "Never let the birds out," he ordered. "They've got permanent injuries and they can't hunt. In the wild, they'd die."

"Sir, yes, sir." Right then, I came up with the perfect name for Lucas. *Sergeant Bird Nerd.*

Two brown and white owls stared down at him from a perch. I ducked, sure Lucas was a dead man. But the birds stayed put, blinking round dark eyes. "What do you know about northern spotted owls?" he asked while he cleaned the mew.

"I know they have spots . . . *Sergeant.*" I whispered the last word.

"Obviously. Also, they're endangered. Their territory's shrinking, and barred owls are moving into what's left."

"Barred owls?" I echoed. "What the heck are those?"

"They look like spotteds, only they have brown stripes—bars—across their chest instead of spots. Their hoot sounds like someone saying, 'Who cooks for you?'"

"Hilarious," I muttered.

"Not really. Now that they've migrated west, the old growth forest's getting pretty crowded."

Like the ocean. Once, Manhattan Beach got some heinous riptides, and their surfers moved in on Redondo Beach waves. The ocean was so packed I could barely surf.

"Daydreamer, huh?" Lucas stretched rubber gloves over his hands. "Listen up. First, we pick up all the parts."

"Parts?"

"Chicken feet, mouse heads, rat tails. Anything the birds don't eat."

"*Gross!*"

Lucas dropped a pair of orange chicken feet into the bucket. "Hey, kid—raptors can't live on vegetables and tofu. They eat meat. Ours are too damaged to hunt on their own, so we give them food that's already dead."

My left hand reached to cover my bandaged wrist.

"Here." Lucas poked an inch-long grayish white *thing* through the wire.

I jumped back. "What is that?"

Not a paw. Please, not a paw.

"Owl pellet. Owls eat their prey whole. But they can't digest some of it, so their stomach makes a pellet. Indigestible bones on the inside, fur and feathers on the outside. They cough it up. Break the pellet open—you'll see what these owls had for dinner."

I looked down and saw a tiny skull embedded in the pellet. My stomach went belly-up. Somewhere on my parents' acre, there was a pellet full of kitten bones. I hurled the thing far into the forest.

Lucas narrowed his eyes. "Gotta understand the birds if you're gonna help them." He pushed through the door with his bucket and turned the key in the padlock. "There's the hose. Wash the feathers off the sides of the enclosure and spray the poop into the gravel." He handed me the bucket. I couldn't look inside.

"We'll do Artemis next. She goes quickly because we can't go into her enclosure."

"*We?*" No way was I getting within ten feet of an owl. Sergeant Bird Nerd could pick up rat tails by himself.

Lucas shrugged. "It's this or juvenile corrections, kid. You make the choice."

"Whatever." I locked my jaw and stomped after him to the mew half covered with a blue tarp. It looked empty.

"Has Minerva told you about Artemis?" He didn't wait for me to answer. "Raised illegally by humans. She's an imprint—too much contact with people when she was a baby."

He scratched his scalp. A white feather fell out and drifted to his shoulder. "She thinks we're her species. Can't go into her enclosure because she's scared we'll steal her territory. Only Minerva's allowed inside—Artemis thinks she's her mate. If anyone else went in, she'd try to kill them."

He unlocked the door to the entryway between us and the mew. "Once, a volunteer thought he was tough and went into her enclosure. I've never heard anything like his scream. His arm was shredded."

The scabs on my wrist ached. "So where *is* this killer bird?"

"Sitting on eggs." Again, Lucas studied me, then picked up a hose. "I'll call her out so you can see her."

"I don't want . . ." I began, but he aimed a spray of mist through the mew door toward the perch.

"Solo, meet Artemis."

There's a moment in *The Birds* when Hitchcock pans in on crows swarming a schoolyard. A group of crows is actually called a *murder* of crows. You can tell from the terror on actress Tippi Hedren's face that she knows just why they're labeled with that name. I felt her same panic when an enormous great horned owl rose up to the perch in front of me.

She stood twice as big as Hermes. Vengeful, yellow eyes locked onto mine. She unfurled her wings—they were almost as wide as I was tall. I stared at her feet—tawny feathers led to curved black talons, each two inches long and poised to kill.

83

The world spun. Again, I heard my kitten mewing, the hideous screech . . . I saw the furry gray and white body. My breath tangled in my lungs, threatened to choke me.

"She loves to get a shower," Lucas said.

Oblivious to the fact that his latest at-risk youth was about to pass out, Lucas continued spraying cold water over Artemis. Slowly, the owl's ear tufts dropped, and she stretched out her wings. With one wing tilted up, Artemis looked like a woman ready to scrub her armpit.

But she was the enemy—my sworn foe. I glared at the bird. She blinked back at me.

"If she can fly, Minerva should let her go."

Lucas snapped to attention. "She never learned to hunt. She'd *die* in the wild."

His eyebrow lowered in a furious V, just like the black feathers over Artemis's eyes. "*Never* raise a wild animal as a pet. Tame it, and you hand it a death sentence."

I thought again of my kitten and swallowed hard against the tightness in my throat. "I'm never gonna have another pet."

Artemis ruffled up her feathers and clacked her beak—the same beak that she used to rip apart small, helpless animals. "Especially not a *bird*."

Lucas turned off the hose. Three long scars gleamed white against his tanned arm. "Yeah? We'll wait and see."

I dropped the bucket and stalked away toward the clinic. *You'll be waiting a long, long time, Sergeant Bird Nerd.*

Chapter Seven
FREEDOM OF MOBILITY

Solo, fold the laundry! Mop the floors! Weed the butterfly garden!"

Now I knew why Lucas supervised at-risk kids at the raptor center. The guy put the *D* in dictator.

"He's a fantastic artist," Minerva told me. "When I first met him, he was a teenager spray painting graffiti on buildings. Now he's getting an art degree. Have you seen his sketches?"

I shook my head. No way was I getting friendly with Sergeant Bird Nerd. He jabbered on and on about raptors like there was nothing else in the world. We'd be knee-deep in bird poop and suddenly, he'd bust out with a lecture.

"Peregrine falcons can fly two hundred sixty miles an hour, straight down. They ball up their talons and knock their prey out cold in midair," Lucas told me once.

"Good for them," I'd mutter.

I'd have my head in a water trough, scrubbing out green algae at Lucas's command, and he'd start up again.

"Know why vultures don't have feathers on their heads, kid? They pick at flesh inside rotting carcasses. Bald heads are easier to keep clean."

"Then maybe you should lose the ponytail," I whispered.

But I had to do what he said. It was this or juvenile corrections . . . *kid*.

Friday afternoon, Lucas ordered me to water Minerva's butterfly garden while he fed the pygmy owls. Lucas gave them each a thawed chick, then turned to me. "Owls can tell the location of their prey in total darkness 'cause they have lopsided ears."

"Good thing they don't wear earrings," I retorted.

That day, I swiped another postcard from the office and taped an inch-long pellet to the back.

Hey, Raj—
Check out this screech owl pellet. They hack up stuff
they can't digest. Wish I could hack up my mom's tofu.

Stay cool,
Solo

Rajen would freak when he saw it. No owl pellets on the beach.

Lucas looked up from cleaning Hermes's mew. "Hey, kid, how'd you get here?"

My stomach lurched. Hadn't Minerva told him? "Uh . . . an owl murdered my kitten, and I accidentally shot . . ."

"No, how'd you get to the center today? Parents drop you off?"

I jerked my chin at my skateboard propped next to his red road bike.

He whistled. "That's a wild ride down the mountain. Potholes, rocks . . . pretty dangerous way to travel."

I shrugged. "Four wheels is better than none."

"I've got an extra bike," he said. "It's yours if you want it."

"For free?" I squinted at him. "What's the catch?"

Lucas scowled. "No catch. It's not my bike. Carrie— my ex-girlfriend—was about your size. I've gotta drive my truck Monday to load up the garbage, so I'll toss the bike in the back and bring it here."

A used bike. I'd never taken someone's hand-me-downs. If I wanted something, my parents bought it new. But Voluntary Simplicity, according to my parents, meant reduce, reuse, and recycle. I knew they'd never buy me a new bike now.

"D'you give stuff to *all* the at-risk kids?" I asked Lucas.

"Look, if you don't want it, just say so."

I studied my skateboard. One of the wheels wobbled like a loose tooth. "Doesn't Carrie need her bike?"

Lucas lowered his eyebrow. "She moved to Florida." He slammed out the door with a plate of fish. "I'm gonna be up feeding the eagles."

"See you next week!" I yelled. He didn't answer.

Inside his clean mew, Hermes ruffled his feathers and clacked his beak.

"Betcha Carrie broke Sergeant Bird Nerd's heart," I whispered.

The owl bobbed his head. Obviously, he agreed.

•

There's always a catch when something's free. On Monday, Lucas pulled up in his truck with a blue mountain bike—knobby tires and a black lightning bolt streaking across the frame, just a little rusty. I didn't mind the rust. But I sure minded the pink plastic pig's head welded onto the handlebar. I pushed its nose. It squeaked.

"Well . . ." Edgar said from her mew. "Ha ha ha ha!"

"What's up with the pig?" I asked Lucas.

"It's a horn. You squeak the pig to tell people you're behind them."

"I know *that*. How do you get it off?"

"You don't. The bike comes as is."

I stared at him, sure he was joking. But Lucas never joked.

"You're telling me I can't have the bike unless I keep the pig?" I said.

"Correct."

"You put that pig on there to make fun of me."

Lucas pulled on a pair of leather gloves. "Lighten up, kid."

Minerva met us in the driveway. "Good morning, Solo. Lucas is helping me trim beaks today. You can clean the down off the mews."

"*All* of them?"

The fluffy down feathers clung to everything, stubborn as beach tar on bare feet. No spraying it off with the hose—it just stuck worse.

"Can't we leave it there? It's not hurting anything," I argued.

Minerva looked at Lucas with a little smile twisting on her lips. He nodded and turned to me. "That would look pretty sloppy. Visitors need to see clean enclosures and birds that are well cared for."

"Whatever." I snatched up a bucket and stomped off. "Thirty freakin' mews. This is *worse* than jail."

It took me hours to clean all the mews. I finished all the hawks and falcons, the vultures and the osprey. Finally, I moved on to the owls. Artemis rustled on her nest behind the tarp. Lucas told me her eggs wouldn't hatch. Artemis had never been with a male great horned owl. "But females automatically lay eggs once a year," he said. So here she was trying to coax babies out of a bunch of lifeless shells, like a surfer trying to ride flat water. I almost felt sorry for her.

Almost.

I picked the down off the screech owl mew and turned on the hose to soak the flowers. With a flutter of wings, Artemis loomed up on her wooden perch and glared at me from yellow eyes. Ear tufts jutted, and talons bit into wood. Fear gripped my throat.

But the owl curled one foot up into her breast feathers and blinked at the water streaming out of the hose. She clacked her beak.

"You . . . you want a *shower?*"

I studied the wire around her mew. No way could she escape. She ruffled up her feathers. "It's called *rousing*," I heard Sergeant Bird Nerd say in my head. "Helps birds to clean off their feathers and realign them more neatly."

I aimed the hose up toward the sky. Water droplets pattered down on my face and arms. Artemis spread out her wings and clacked her beak again.

"So, you've befriended our venerable great horned owl," Minerva said beside me.

I whipped the hose toward the flower garden. "No way!"

"Ever notice she's paler than Hermes?" Minerva unlocked the padlock and stepped into the enclosure with a bucket. I held my breath, but Artemis only chirped at her.

"Eastern birds have to camouflage with snow. She's from Philadelphia. Sometimes I think that's why she's so moody. She misses her home."

What I wouldn't give to stand with my feet in hot sand again, waves crashing around me.

"Two o'clock." Minerva tapped her watch. "I'll finish cleaning this one."

I looked around. The golden eagles preened in the sun. Above them, the balds sat up straight, lording over the smaller birds below. The osprey splashed and screeched in her water trough.

Back in the trailer, I'd hide in the sweltering cave of my bedroom, listening to my father pound his type-writer—or worse, not touch it at all—while my mother concocted tofu-surprise in the kitchen with that new angry crack between her eyebrows.

I cleared my throat. "Uh . . . Minerva? I can stay a while longer."

"Wonderful."

Behind the tarp, Minerva bent to examine the eggs. Artemis stayed put on her perch.

"Um . . . my dad wants to know how you got your name," I mumbled. "He says it's classical or something."

"I changed it when I moved here. Minerva's a Roman goddess, often depicted with an owl. How'd you get yours?"

I told her about my mother's fascination with *Star Wars*. She stood up and brushed her hands off on her jeans. "Solo. The one and only."

She got busy picking up parts then, and I went back to work. Artemis watched while I plucked the down off another owl mew. But when I headed for the clinic an hour later, she was back on those eggs. Maybe having a job took her mind off being homesick.

Minerva's station wagon sat outside the clinic, a purple bumper sticker plastered across her back window. FOLLOW YOUR BLISS, it read. What's that *mean?*

Lucas walked out of the clinic, swinging a bike helmet. He thumped the hard plastic. "Wear it, kid. It'll save you from brain injury if you endo."

"Endo?"

"End over. Go head over heels."

"Who said I'm gonna take your bike?"

Lucas looped the helmet straps over the handlebar. "Suit yourself. But you can't beat a bicycle for freedom of mobility."

Freedom.

Cyclists rode down the Pacific Coast Highway in California all the time. We'd passed a bunch of them, their bicycles hung with big black bags, the day we moved.

I studied the bike. How long would it take me to ride back to Redondo Beach?

"Lucas, come help me tube feed this hawk!" Minerva called.

"Catch you later, Solo."

I waited until Sergeant Bird Nerd went inside, then wheeled the bike down the driveway to Eyrie Road. I swung my backpack over my shoulders. It hit the pig, and the stupid thing squeaked.

Edgar flew up to her perch and laughed. I ignored her. "Here goes nothing. . . ."

I pushed off and coasted down the hill. Trees blurred green. A cool wind whipped my face, and the knobby tires sailed over rocks that would have meant death on a skateboard.

"Woo-hoo!" I let out a long whoop and flew past the bus stop. Kids stared at me, openmouthed. "So long, suckers!" I yelled.

Riding up the hill felt like torture. I stood up and dug my heels into the pedals hard. Halfway up, I had to surrender. My heart whacked against my ribs as I jogged, pushing the bike beside me. A few more workouts like this and cycling a thousand miles back to Redondo Beach would be no problem.

At the mailboxes, I stuck my hand in and pulled out a fat envelope that read: WELCOME HOME—VALUABLE COUPONS ENCLOSED! I reached in again to pull out a letter from Dad's doctor and a postcard from Rajen—a picture of the ocean at sunset.

Hey, Solo,
Get a computer already! Don't forget Operation Surf's Up. Got carpet in tree house and my bro's old dorm room fridge. We can have root beer floats, dude!

Your friend,
Rajen

Soon, I'd be riding into that golden sunset, far away from my alien parents. I could almost taste the vanilla ice cream melting into my root beer; hear my friends cracking up over some dumb joke.

My legs felt like limp, rubbery seaweed as I staggered up the driveway. The bandage slipped down on my sweaty wrist. The three long scabs had almost healed, so I ripped the thing off with my teeth and crumpled it into my pocket.

Lucas had ordered me to wipe the bike down after every ride to prevent rust. I leaned it against the shed behind the trailer and scraped thick grease off the chain and gears, then rubbed the frame with an old rag. Just enough room for a Billabong surfing decal. As I worked, I thought about that bumper sticker on Minerva's car. FOLLOW YOUR BLISS.

Bliss. It means something you love to do. But how could I follow my bliss in Oregon?

Impossible.

I wheeled the bike into the shed and closed the door.

CHAPTER EIGHT
WHAT NEXT?

The next day, I flew through my community service hours and rode downtown, weaving through the streets until I found a bike shop.

"Help you find something?" A skinny guy in spandex bike shorts looked up from a bicycle on a stand and walked over to me, wiping his hands on an apron.

"I'm looking for those big black bags. The kind you put on your bike."

"They're called panniers." He studied my bike, made no comment on the squeaky pig. "You'll need a pair of them and a rack over your back tire. Oh, and don't you want some fenders for the rainy season?"

I shook my head. By the time the rain hit Oregon, I'd be kicking back in Rajen's tree house and homeschooling on the waves. "How much are the bags?" I hefted the two he handed me—sturdy black cases the size of grocery bags, each with a silver reflective strip. Metal hooks on one side affixed the panniers to the rack he pulled down from the wall.

"They're fifty dollars each. Where're you touring?"

"Uh . . ." I hesitated. Didn't want to give away too much information. I'd watched enough television to know that if I ran away on a bicycle, the police would storm the bike shops first and demand to know whether I'd been in, whether I'd revealed any small detail about Operation Surf's Up. I set the panniers on the glass counter by the cash register. "I'll be back in soon. Thanks for your help."

I rode to the library crunching numbers in my head. My Darth Vader bank held $45.80. If I could persuade my parents to give me five dollars a week in allowance (five, when I used to earn twenty), I could buy a couple of panniers and be back in Redondo Beach before the end of summer.

My parents wouldn't miss me. Would they even know I was gone?

They barely spoke to each other or to me. Dinner sucked—it was tofu-surprise at the miniscule table in the trailer, and all I could hear was chewing . . . *my* chewing, since they only pushed food around on their plates and stared into space.

What the heck were they searching for?

"Your dad's got writer's block again," Mom whispered as we washed the dishes. Then I got that he was searching for words—my father, who talked like *Webster's Dictionary.*

But what was my mother looking for? I locked my bike and sprinted up the library steps, trying to forget the look in her eyes . . . both hunting and haunted.

In the library's little computer room full of people bent over their borrowed keyboards, Rajen's email stabbed like talons into my gut.

Hey, dude!
A tenth grader just moved into your house. His name's Eldon—he surfed twenty-foot waves in Hawaii. He's super cool. We're using the tree house as a crash pad till you get back.

Raj

Not "Stay Cool, Rajen" or "Your Friend, Rajen." Suddenly, he was "Raj," and not one word about Operation Surf's Up. I jammed my finger against the delete button and hurtled down the staircase, skidding on the slick surface of the library lobby.

"Hey, watch out!" A cute little kid with wild brown curls tried to dodge me and dropped an armload of books about dragons.

"Sorry." I helped her pick up the books and take them to the checkout counter, then flung myself onto my bike and rode toward the river.

Slumped on a bench, I stared out at the duck pond. Dozens of mallards and gray and white geese floated around. Some of their wings stuck out permanently at weird angles—ANGEL WING, I read on a sign near the pond, caused by too much bread. I wondered if anyone was helping them the way Minerva helped birds of prey.

I reached into my backpack and pulled out the Altoids tin Rajen had given me that last day in Redondo Beach. I poured the sand into my palm and licked a shell with the tip of my tongue. The taste of salt had almost vanished.

Someone's taken over my territory. If I had talons, I thought, *I'd rip this Eldon's surfboard to shreds.*

I tossed the tin into a trash can and rode home, trying to convince myself that my eyes watered from sweat.

Eric stood in the driveway with a long-handled net and a jar. "I like your Pig Wheel!" He squeaked the pig on my handlebar. "Wanna catch bugs?"

"I have an appointment." I pressed my palms against my eyes to block him from my view. "And it's not a Pig Wheel," I muttered, annoyed because he'd come up with the perfect name for my bike.

"Appointment?" I looked up at the sudden worry in his voice. He cupped his fingers around his jaw, brow furrowed like one of those wrinkly dogs. "You go to dentist?"

"Sort of."

My mother stepped onto the trailer porch. "The VW's fixed, so we don't have to rush to the bus stop." She lowered her voice. "Your father's not feeling well.

Why don't you play with your friend outside till it's time to see your social worker."

"*Mom!*" I groaned, but it was hopeless. In one sentence, the Alien Mother had fired three deadly blasts straight at me.

Bzzzzt! Fourteen-year-olds don't *play*.

Bzzzzt! Why'd she have to tell him about my social worker?

Bzzzzt! Eric wasn't my friend. I had no friends since Eldon moved into my tree house.

Eric didn't notice any of this. He had bugs on the brain.

"Solo! Look. A lacewing." He held out a jar with a top that magnified stuff inside.

I sighed and dropped my backpack. "Let me see." A green-winged bug sat on a blade of grass. Up close, its wings had all these lines, like the loopy patterns on a sand dollar. "That's pretty cool."

Eric opened the lid and let the lacewing fly free. We watched it fly off toward my mom's square of dirt, home to a couple of carrots and a wilted zucchini plant. "My mother and me go hiking Saturday. You wanna come?"

"I guess."

Nothing I did mattered anymore.

Mom appeared again on the porch, jangling her keys. "You're welcome to come into town with us," she told Eric. "We can get raw-veggie smoothies while Solo talks with his social worker."

Bzzzzt!

I shot Mom the evil eye. She shot it right back.

Eric shook his head. "I want to catch dragonflies!" He waved his net. "See you Saturday, Solo. Hope you don't have cavities!"

"What's he talking about?" Mom shook out her gauzy hippie skirt and untangled one dangly beaded earring from her braid.

I dragged myself up into The Big Grape. Above me, a red-tailed hawk perched on the telephone pole, preparing for a dinner date with some innocent mouse.

Mom's lecture started before we hit the road. "You should be nice to Eric. He doesn't have any friends."

Neither do I.

I closed my eyes. For an instant, Rajen and I stood on the beach again, surfboards under our arms and sun baking our shoulders. But then some hotshot surfer rode a twenty-foot wave into shore, and my best friend vanished into the fog.

"Solo, I'm talking to you!"

I swallowed the lump in my throat. "Mom, I just caught bugs with Eric for half an hour. What else do you want from me?"

The Big Grape groaned, catching sight of the hill. I pressed my hands against my aching thighs. I knew from biking just how it felt.

"You act like you're better than him," Mom snapped.

"I do not!"

But she was right. Even though Eric was a year older than me, he reminded me of Rajen's little brother—a pest, an embarrassment, always showing up at the wrong time.

"It's not his fault he's different." The ice in Mom's voice melted a little. "He needs our support. Imagine what you could teach him about the ocean, Solo. That kid's a real nature lover."

"I'll think about it," I mumbled.

"I'd appreciate that."

One lecture over, she started another. "Your social worker's going to be pleased with your progress."

"Progress?"

"Don't get defensive. I simply mean you seem to be enjoying your work with the birds. You're making fine progress."

Until she dragged me to Oregon, I'd washed the dishes and taken out the trash without being told. I never ditched school or smoked. And I didn't lie, even when Eric's father got in my face and screamed, "Did you fire my shotgun?"

But *progress* meant there was a problem—something wrong with me.

"What exactly have I progressed from?" Sergeant Bird Nerd's precise, prissy voice came out of my mouth.

Mom looked sideways at me. She didn't say the words. She didn't have to.

My chest tightened, and my eyes stung again. "I'm *not* a criminal! *I'm* the one who got straight A's last year, the one who cleaned the house and cooked for everyone when Dad was in the hospital, remember? *I'm* the one who cleans poop and chicken feet out of bird mews all day. So I shot a gun *one time*! It was a mistake. Why can't you leave me alone!"

"Don't yell at me!" Mom's voice ricocheted off the windshield. "You have no idea what I'm up against. First your father goes crazy, then you? What next, Solo? What next?"

A minute later, she got her answer. Because right at the top of the hill, The Big Grape died again.

Mom and I glared at each other. The bus rolled backwards, and she yanked up the parking brake. Gray exhaust billowed around us. There was nothing else around but trees and dirt.

"Maybe it just needs a rest," I choked. "Give it a minute."

And then my mother did something I'd seen only once before, on the afternoon my father tried to off himself. She burst into tears.

"I'm so tired of this!" she wailed. "Always breaking down, always something wrong. No good piece of . . . *crap*!" She slapped the dashboard like she was giving the Grape a spanking. "I hate the country. I miss my friends. I miss my job. I want my mother!"

I pictured my grandmother in her big house with the manicured bushes and the palm trees and the swimming pool out back. We'd left her along with everything else. Mom hadn't seemed to care. But now, she covered her face with her hands and bowed her head until it lay against the steering wheel.

"It's okay," I said. "Dad'll get the bus to start."

"Ha! Your father couldn't tell a spark plug from a carrot, even if he could get up the nerve to leave the house." She lifted her head and smacked the dashboard again. "I miss my Corvette!"

My jaw dropped to my chest, and my eyes bugged out. I must have looked like one of Dad's cartoons because Mom stared at me, and suddenly, she started laughing like a maniac.

"I miss my Corvette!" she howled. "Yikes. Looks like we're having a couple of nervous breakdowns to rival your father's." She looked at me, really looked at me for a moment, and the hard look in her eyes softened. "I'm sorry. What say we ditch this dinosaur, hike home, and order a pizza."

"Fine with me." I jumped out of the bus and we headed down the shoulder, in the shade of tall trees.

Lucas told me they were called Douglas firs. "Not all evergreens are *pines*, kid," he'd said.

Mom took my hand. "You're a good son, Solo. I should tell you that more often."

Her hand felt sweaty, too hot. As soon as I could, I knelt to remove a pretend rock from my shoe. I didn't need her to hold my hand, to remind me that I was good. I just didn't want her to think I was bad.

"Let's run home!" Mom's voice shot up an octave, the way it did when I had the flu two years ago and a temperature so high we went to the ER. "We'll pretend we're jogging on the beach. Remember what that felt like—all that sand as far as you could see . . . the crash of waves . . . how wonderful the water felt on your bare feet?"

I remembered.

We began to jog. Trees turned into lifeguard stands, and vultures became seagulls swooping overhead. Did my mother also see pelicans bobbing on the ocean instead of sheep grazing in the field near our acreage?

Now I knew she missed California. But we'd sold our house and this kid Eldon, Rajen's new best friend, was living it up in my big bedroom with an ocean view.

If we move back, is there even a place for me anymore?

We staggered up to the trailer's porch, sweaty and panting. Dad lay on the couch with a washcloth over his face. Mom spent half an hour on the phone, looking for someone who'd deliver a pizza all the way out to the trailer. She finally found a place, but Dad didn't eat a bite even though we'd ordered his favorite—pineapple and Canadian bacon. "Just this once." Mom picked the ham off her slices and laid them on my pizza like a peace offering.

That night in bed, I chowed on leftovers and worked on a new screenplay scene.

WHAT NEXT?

FADE IN
EXTERIOR. OLD TRAILER - NIGHT.

SOLO HAHN sits cross-legged in the grass with a bug net beside him. He stares up at the sky.

CLOSE-UP of a falling star. Eyes closed, Solo makes a wish.

                    SOLO
     I wish I was home, back at the beach
     with my surfboard.

Suddenly, headlights sweep across his face. A new black Corvette races up the gravel driveway, CD player blaring big band music. MOM and DAD step through a cloud of dust toward their son.

                    SOLO
     You bought a new car?

                    DAD
     This is more our style, don't you think?

Solo nods. Mom reaches to take his hand, pulls him up to stand beside her.

MOM
You were right, sweetie. Let's go home.

SOLO
What about the trailer?

DAD
We're leaving this sorry piece of
tin behind.

SOLO
I . . .

I couldn't finish the scene that night. Maybe Dad's writer's block was contagious.

I turned off the light and stared out the window. Overhead, billions of stars twinkled, each one glowing with the promise of its own separate wish. The moon shined the tops of the fir trees with silver. Deep within the forest, I heard the searching call of a great horned owl.

It seemed to cry: *what next?*

Chapter Nine
EAT DESSERT FIRST

The clack of typewriter keys woke me at seven. Then silence.

"If you're not going to write, you could at least get a job!" My mother's voice yanked my head up off the pillow. "I woke up early to make breakfast so you could write. And now, you're not even working!"

My father made a sound—a syllable between a word and a whimper. More silence. Then, I heard glass shatter.

I leapt out of bed.

"These damn colleges want to pay me *one-third* of what I made in California. We're living on our savings so you can write your novel, and now you're not writing? Honestly, Michael, I don't know what to do for you!"

A door slammed. Footsteps pounded toward the kitchen.

I tiptoed out of my room. My parents' flimsy wooden door stayed shut. Down the hall, I saw Mom hunched over the stove. I crept silently back into my room, read a chapter of *One Man's Owl*, and then decided to venture out to the kitchen.

"G'morning." I sat down at the table like everything was fine, like my guts weren't writhing with fear.

Mom's eyes looked red and painful. She banged the jar of spiced apples on the table and slid a couple blackened buckwheat pancakes onto my plate. "It's a hundred degrees in this stupid trailer." She twisted her hair on top of her head and jabbed a barrette through the mess.

"It never got hot in Redondo Beach." I mentioned this casually, like I was just making conversation instead of trying desperately to find out whether were headed back down south. "The breeze kept stuff cool."

But my mother only shrugged and turned back to the stove with her shoulders hunched over the griddle.

Now Dad shuffled out in his happy face T-shirt and boxers, topped by a gray silk kimono. His hair stuck up like a baby bird's. He wandered toward the coffee pot and sloshed himself a cupful. Then he sprawled on the couch and turned on National Public Radio.

"Can you listen to that later?" Mom snapped.

He looked over, blinked. "I'm researching the human condition."

I knew better. Dad looked just like a sick bird slumped in a plastic pet carrier.

How do you rehabilitate a suffering dad?

I picked up the bottle of pills on his place mat. "Michael Hahn—Take one a day for anxiety." Antidepressants.

"They help to heal someone who's clinically depressed," Mom told me too loudly. "But they don't work unless you actually *take* them."

My father called over from the couch, "I told you, I don't feel like myself when I take that stuff."

"Maybe that's a good thing," Mom shot back.

I closed my eyes. Again, I saw Dad's limp body laid out on the stretcher.

I put down the pill bottle and cut the burned parts off my pancakes.

A truck rattled up the driveway. Mrs. Miller. I spied Eric hanging out the car's window with his magnifying glass held to one eye.

"What're they doing here?" Mom reached into her shorts pocket for her lipstick.

"I'm going hiking," I mumbled.

"With *Eric*?"

I leapt up and rinsed my plate. This morning, I would've gone hiking with Sergeant Bird Nerd if it meant escaping the trailer and my sad father. Just look-ing at him made me want to cry.

"You're not hiking in sports sandals. It's poison oak season," Mom said.

I shrugged. "I don't have hiking boots."

Mom disappeared down the hall and came back with a pair of black Montrails.

"I got these at Goodwill last week. They're just your size."

I picked the boots up by their laces. *Used.* Scuff marks marred the toes. Flecks of mud spattered the bottom. "What if the guy these belonged to sees me and wants them back?"

Mom rolled her eyes. "Honestly, Solo. Remember the three *R*s? Reduce, reuse, recycle."

Ridiculous.

I ducked her finger full of sunscreen, dropped the boots, and ran out to the truck. Eric opened the door. "Yay! Solo's coming!"

Mom followed me out, Montrails in hand. "It's so beautiful out today . . . too gorgeous to stay inside."

Together, we looked back through the screen door to where Dad lay on the couch. The metal sides of the trailer held heat inside like an oven. He looked like he was being baked alive.

Mrs. Miller waved to Mom from the driver's seat. "Come with us, honey."

A smile flashed across my mother's face. For a moment, her eyes shone. "Oh, I'd love to."

"Mom," I whispered. "We can't leave him alone. Who knows *what* he'll do."

In an instant, her face clouded. "You're right."

"I'd better stay here," she called out to Mrs. Miller, too cheerfully. "I haven't even checked the employment ads this morning."

"Another day, then."

Mrs. Miller started up the truck. I took the boots from my mother.

110

"Thanks," I muttered.

Out the window, I waved. With her red lipstick and her hair swept up to show off the diamond earrings my father had given her on their tenth anniversary, she didn't look like she belonged in front of a decrepit trailer in the middle of Oregon.

Slowly, she raised her hand and waved good-bye. Then she turned and went inside.

Mrs. Miller gunned the truck up the hill and headed for Eyrie Road. "You'll love the view from the top of Spencer Butte," she told me. "It's worth the climb."

Spencer Butte was the mountain that hovered above the raptor center. If people around here got lost, they used the butte for direction, like sailors use the North Star. Only the butte lay south of the city.

"Why's it called a butte?" I asked Mrs. Miller. "When I first moved here, I thought it was pronounced 'butt.'"

Eric giggled. His mom smiled and brushed her sweaty bangs off her forehead. "The way I learned it, if it's got friends, then it's a mountain. But if it's a mountain with no other mountains around, it's a by-itself butte. Get it?"

Rajen's last email—all about his new best friend—flashed across my mind.

"I get it."

Mrs. Miller parked in a lot across from the raptor center, near a sign warning hikers of rattlesnakes and cougars. "Never seen one yet." She threw a backpack over her shoulders and led us across the road to a dirt path.

"Ha ha ha ha!" Edgar's voice rang out. Fifty feet up, I saw her mew half hidden by trees and ferns.

Can she sense I'm here?

Eric threw himself down on a wooden bridge across a barely trickling creek. "Wanna see water striders!" He peered through his magnifying glass.

I studied the rink of long-legged bugs skating on top of the water. But Mrs. Miller had her heart set on summiting the butte. "C'mon, boys." She fanned her face with her hat. "Let's see what kind of insects live at the top."

We climbed, stopping at least once every minute so Eric could identify a new tree. "Douglas fir!" He grabbed a limb of one dangling branch and shook it like a hand. Then he ran to a tree with purple flowers. "Plum!" He smiled his wide happy smile. "Birds eat plums, then poop the seeds. They make a plum tree!"

I pretended to gag. "Gross!"

Mrs. Miller laughed. "I swear my son's gonna be the next John Muir."

"John who?"

"John Muir was a writer who helped protect Yosemite National Park in California. He's my hero."

She stood up straight and sucked in a deep breath like she was about to give an oral report. "'Climb the mountains and get their good tidings. Nature's peace will flow into you as sunshine flows into trees. The winds will blow their own freshness into you . . . while cares will drop off like autumn leaves.' John Muir wrote that. It's pretty, don'tcha think?"

I nodded. Eric stuck a piece of green plant to my shirt. "Bedstraw. Pioneer people stuffed their beds with it."

"Their mattresses," his mother explained.

"That's cool." I fell into step behind him. "You really do know a lot about nature, Eric."

"Yup."

The path veered right, straight up the face of the butte. My calf muscles burned as I climbed over boulders, and my heartbeat banged in my ears. Finally, Mrs. Miller stopped climbing and collapsed under a pine tree.

"Welcome to Oregon!" she cried.

There's a scene in an old movie called *Dead Poets Society* where Robin Williams tells his students to stand on their desks. "The world looks very different from up here," he says. "Just when you think you know something, you have to look at it in another way."

Mr. Davies showed us the movie in screenwriting class. Then he told us to stand on *our* desks. The only thing I saw differently was dust on the fluorescent bulb above my head. But here on Spencer Butte, I understood what Robin Williams and Mr. Davies were getting at. The sky glowed blue over forests stretched far as I could see. To the right, I glimpsed the glimmer of a lake. In the distance, three mountains huddled together.

"The Three Sisters," Mrs. Miller told me as I pointed to the trio of mountains. "Volcanoes, part of the Cascade

Volcanic Arc. This is an amazing state, Solo. Mountains, forests, pristine lakes perfect for summer swimming, beaches full of sea stacks . . ."

"Sea stacks?"

"They're these tall rock formations that jut up from the ocean. You can see them up and down the coast. Don't you have them in Southern California?"

"I don't think so."

I looked out at the Sisters and, for a moment, my parents and their moods and their problems didn't matter. Nature's peace flowed into me, and I smiled.

"That's our city." Mrs. Miller pointed to a cluster of Monopoly-sized buildings plopped down among millions of trees. Somewhere, my father lay on the couch in the middle of all that green.

The wind blew into the firs and pines around us. It made a sound I recognized, but couldn't place. I closed my eyes.

The ocean. The wind sounds like the ocean.

I looked up. A dark-winged bird circled above our heads, dipping down, then soaring high.

"That bird's catching a thermal," I told Eric. "That's a column of warm air. Birds float on thermals like surfers ride waves."

I thought the bird was a vulture. But then it swooped closer, and the sun gleamed against its white head feathers.

"It's a bald eagle!" I shouted.

Eric peered through his binoculars. Mrs. Miller clapped her hand over her heart. "Our national bird!"

I watched the eagle float on the wind. "Did you guys know Ben Franklin wanted our national bird to be the turkey?"

"Turkey?" Eric shrieked with laughter. "Good one, Solo!"

I recalled what Sergeant Bird Nerd had told me. "Nature made the bald eagle's feet without feathers, so it can fish. Otherwise, it'd be flying around in feathers that felt like wet socks."

The idea of a raptor in footwear got Eric giggling even harder.

Mrs. Miller unzipped her backpack. "I had no idea you knew so much about birds, honey." She pulled out peanut butter, bread, and bananas. Then she took out a big bag of chocolate chip cookies.

When I saw those cookies, I almost cried. Eric grabbed one and chomped it down. Mrs. Miller caught me staring and handed me two. "Here, Solo. Life's unpredictable—better eat dessert first."

I stuffed them both in my mouth at once and nodded my thanks. She laughed.

Around us, lizards did push-ups on mossy rocks. Birds swooped from tree to tree. Eric swapped his binoculars for a magnifying glass and leaned down to study a beetle while his mother sliced bananas for our sandwiches. With my mouth full of cookies, I had to work hard to keep feeling like a lonely butte.

Maybe Mrs. Miller understood a little about how I was feeling. "We're gonna head down," she said after lunch, packing up wrappers and banana peels.

I picked up a napkin and stuffed it in my pocket. "Do you . . . do you mind if I stay a few minutes?" I asked her. "By myself? I just want to see what it's like to be up here alone."

She studied me for a moment, then nodded. "You stay as long as you want. We'll wait for you on the trail where it forks into two."

She climbed down the boulders with Eric and disappeared into the trees.

I stood up and climbed to the highest point on the butte, a pinnacle on a pile of boulders.

Above me, the eagle kept surfing thermals. I felt like flying, too. What if John Muir was right? What if my father could climb the mountain and get its good tidings? Spencer Butte might just cure him.

I reached for my notebook and pencil.

```
FADE IN
EXTERIOR. MOUNTAINTOP - DAY.
SOLO HAHN stands on top of a butte, arms
stretched wide. A cool breeze ruffles his
hair. In the distance, three snowcapped
volcanic peaks rise into a blue sky.
```

SOLO

See what I mean, Dad? You can't feel
suicidal on the butte.

CLOSE-UP of Solo's father. DAD breathes
deeply and smiles a wide, happy smile.

DAD

You're right, son. Thank you for
bringing me here. I feel positively
exuberant. What say we grab your
mother and go on a backpacking trip,
maybe check out some of those sea
stacks on the coast?

PAN OUT to the eagle soaring over their
heads.

FADE OUT

I slipped my notebook into my pocket and climbed
down the boulders, then ran down the dirt path to catch
up with Mrs. Miller and Eric. He'd stopped to examine
a circle of white flowers through his magnifying glass.
"Queen Anne's Lace."

"Can I see?" I looked through the glass at the tiny
petals, each one perfect, each doing its part to create a
big intricate flower.

I looked at the curly green moss hanging off the tree branches above us. "What's that stuff?"

"*Usnea.* Its common name is Old Man's Beard." Mrs. Miller pulled off a bit of the soft moss and handed it to me. I pulled on one tendril—it stretched between my fingers. "Makes good toilet paper," she added.

"Ew!" Eric and I cried together.

"What d'you think John Muir used when he lived out in the woods? Environmentalists have to live off the land."

"They poop on the land!" Eric high-fived me with his widest smile. Poop or no poop, I liked the idea of living off the land, surviving on blackberries and stream water. *Solo Hahn—Environmentalist.*

The label sounded good in my head.

•

That afternoon, I couldn't wait to get home, to tell Dad all about the butte. Maybe Mom and I could persuade him to hike it with a picnic the next day.

"Where's your mama?" Mrs. Miller stopped in The Big Grape's spot to let me out.

"Yoga?" I guessed. But I walked into the trailer to find my mother in shorts and a T-shirt, slumped at the table with her head buried in her hands.

"You okay, Mom?"

She raised her head and looked at me. Tears streaked her cheeks. She took a deep, shuddering breath. Finally, she spoke.

"Your father's gone."

CHAPTER TEN
ALONE

What d'you mean he's *gone?*"

I glared at my mother. She turned her palms up, helpless. "I went for a jog—just a couple of miles. Came back, and he was gone. There's a note. . . ." Her hand pointed limply toward the hallway.

I ran to the doorway of my parents' room, eyes panning the scene.

INTERIOR. TRAY OF PANCAKES AND GLASS OF ORANGE JUICE ON THE DRESSER; RED ROSE IN A VASE - DAY.

PAN OUT to a checked apron torn down the middle. Shards of shattered coffee mug. Cold coffee pooled on the floor.

CLOSE-UP of a typewriter on the desk, holding a single sheet of paper. SOLO walks over and rips the paper out of the

typewriter. He shivers as he reads the
words out loud.

                    SOLO
    "Failure. Failure. Failure. Failure."

FADE OUT

I fled to my room.

"Dad?" I whispered. I looked under my bed and in
my closet just in case he was playing hide-and-seek with
me like when I was little. But there was only a note,
stuck under my Darth Vader bank. I slumped on the
bed to read it.

Dear Solo,
A father should never abandon his son, I know.
But if I don't go now, temporarily, I'm afraid I might
leave permanently. That would be even more unfair
to you. Be well, and know that you're in my heart
every instant. You are not alone.

Love, Dad

I crumpled up the note and hurled it at Darth Vader. "I
am alone," I muttered.

Slowly, I shuffled out to the kitchen where my
mother still sat with her head in her hands. I poured us

bowls of the weird organic cornflakes she'd bought and splashed in some milk. Then we sat there, not eating. The cereal turned to paste.

"He'll come back," I told her. "He said so in his note."

She nodded, not looking at me.

"I'm going to go clean my room," I said. I had to get away from her. If she hadn't nagged Dad about his writing, he might be lying on the couch right now listening to NPR instead of doing whatever he was doing, wherever he was doing it.

I picked up *One Man's Owl* and forced myself to read. The author's wife got so sick of the bird that she left them both forever. Did *anyone* stay married?

I closed my eyes and contemplated the glowing red inside my eyelids. My mind circled like a vulture around one deadly question.

What if Dad doesn't come back?

•

I slept late Sunday morning and jumped out of bed to scan the driveway. But the VW wasn't there, and my parents' bedroom stood empty. My father hadn't come back.

I heard water running in the bathroom.

"Mom?" I pressed my ear against the closed door. "Everything okay?"

My mother's voice sounded faint, exhausted. "I'm fine, Solo. I'm taking a bath."

"Wanna hike up Spencer's Butte? We could take a picnic . . ."

The door opened. Mom stood in her robe, scowling below her white towel turban. "Don't you have community service today?"

My jaw dropped. "It's . . . it's Sunday."

"Oh. Well, can you go find something to do?"

It's strange how pain works. You can be so scared and sad that it's like you've been gashed open. But then a scab grows over the wound, and later, a scar that makes you even tougher.

Like a robot, I turned away from Mom and walked into the kitchen. I toasted a bagel, buttered it, and wrapped it in foil. Then I jumped on my bike, ignoring the empty parking space by the trailer, and pedaled away.

•

Minerva was loading a large pet carrier into the back of her car as I walked my bike up the steep hill to the center. She didn't seem surprised to see me on a Sunday. "One of our red-tails is sick," she said. "I'm off to the vet. Greet visitors, will you? Give them a map of the center and take their admission fee."

"You *sure* you want me to handle money?"

Minerva climbed into the car. "I wouldn't ask if I wasn't sure."

"Okay." I watched her station wagon disappear down the hill.

Lucas walked out to find me standing on the lawn. "You okay, kid? You look dazed."

I stood up straight. "I'm fine. It's hot."

"How's the bike working out? Hey, long as you're here, can you help me with the injured great horned in the treatment room?"

"No way! That owl could rip my face off."

Lucas shook his head. "He's not an imprint like Artemis. I need you to hold off a vein after I get a blood sample. Leah can hold the owl while I bandage its wing."

"Leah?"

"New volunteer."

"Sounds like you two have it covered."

Sergeant Bird Nerd's eyebrow lowered with disgust. "Geez, Solo. Don't you *want* to help rehabilitate the birds? You could really make a difference here if you'd stop thinking about yourself for two seconds."

He turned and stalked into the office.

I stared after him. My throat stung. I stumbled toward the screen door and opened my mouth to tell him off.

Lucas, you can take this community service gig and . . .

But a girl stood in the clinic. She spoke quietly to Hermes in his little mew, then reached into a dish and offered the owl a wriggling mealworm in her delicate fingers.

"Solo, meet Leah. Leah, Solo." Lucas bent over a clipboard, scribbling.

The girl—Leah—walked over to shake my hand. "Nice to meet you, Solo."

"You, too."

In an instant, I saw how the scene would look on film.

```
FADE IN
INTERIOR. CLINIC - DAY.
```

```
LEAH, about twenty, wears overall shorts
and red high-top sneakers. Sapphire eyes.
A silver hoop gleams in one nostril. She
has a hat pulled over black hair twisted
up in a bun—it's an LA Dodgers cap.
```

```
                SOLO
     Are you from California?
```

```
                LEAH
     Santa Barbara. How'd you know?
```

```
SOLO points to her hat. Leah laughs.
```

```
            LEAH (CONT'D)
     I forgot about that. Are you from LA?
```

```
                SOLO
     Redondo Beach.
```

Leah breaks into a sunny smile.

                    LEAH
    No kidding? My parents live . . .

                    LUCAS
    Are you two gonna stand around gos-
    siping, or can I get some help with
    this owl?

Lucas glared at us through the screen door separating the treatment room from the clinic. "Grab some
gloves, both of you."
Leah smiled. "Oh good, Solo. You're gonna help, too?"
"Uh . . . yeah."
I followed her into the treatment room with its
sheet-covered carriers full of recuperating birds. Lucas
pulled on heavy yellow gloves, then reached into a carrier
and gripped the injured great horned's feathered ankles. He
pulled him out with one quick, decisive movement. "Tuck
in the wings and hold the owl against your chest, like this."
The big brown and black bird squirmed in his arms, its yellow eyes wide. The white patch at its throat fluttered.
Leah pulled on gloves. "You want me
to . . . um . . . take him from you?"
"He won't bite."
The owl hissed and clacked his beak. I thought I
recognized fear gleaming in Leah's eyes. But she reached

for the owl's legs, tucked in his wings, and cradled his body against her chest.

I hovered near the door, ready to run. But the owl didn't fight. He just sat there, pressed up against Leah.

Lucas stretched out the injured wing, unwrapped the pink bandage, and bent down to check the wound.

"What happened to him?" Leah whispered.

"Electrocuted."

According to Minerva, electrocuted birds were usually doomed. They looked good for a few days until the flesh around the wound began to die along with the bird. But this owl had been at the center for months, trying to heal from a wound that wouldn't kill him but wouldn't heal enough for him to go back to the wild.

"He's gonna be fine," Lucas said.

That's when I caught Leah smiling at Lucas. It was the kind of smile I used to see my mom give my dad, like she'd handed him a whole sand dollar. But Sergeant Bird Nerd only had eyes for the owl.

"Here, Solo." He handed me a square of cotton, then stuck a needle into the owl's wing and sucked blood into a syringe. My stomach lurched. "When I say *now*, press the pad down where the needle went in, against the bone. *Firmly*."

He'd asked me to help my enemy. Those talons that could murder a kitten without warning jutted inches from my face. Confusion gripped me.

"*Now!*" Lucas said.

Leah met my eyes over the bird's head. "Now," she said.

I bent and pressed down the cotton pad. My heart banged against my chest.

"What's that noise?" Leah whispered.

Lucas nodded at the owl. "His heartbeat. He's terrified."

She gulped. "That makes two of us."

Lucas turned to me. "Birds bleed a lot, so you've gotta apply pressure for a while to allow the artery to clot."

I pressed down more firmly on the pad.

"You can move closer," Leah said. "I won't bite, either."

The owl lay in her arms, blinking up at us. With one gloved finger, Leah stroked his chest feathers, just once. "If he recovers, will he live here?"

Lucas studied the owl, then shook his head. "Nope. We'll release him at the coast. Two kids found him near the coast there. That's his territory."

"He picked a good one." Leah turned back to me. "Don't you love Oregon, Solo? My parents want me to move back to California after I get my environmental science degree, but I told them no way."

I didn't know what to say to that, so I just breathed in the sharp smell of alcohol Lucas had rubbed on the owl's wing. The bird shifted and clacked his beak. Leah's hands tightened, and the tip of her tongue stuck out between her teeth. The expression reminded me of Eric. Eric reminded me of the trailer, which reminded me of my father and how he'd vanished. What if by the time I biked back that afternoon my mother was gone, too?

•

Leah and I cleaned the down off of all the mews and debated which was better—California or Oregon.

"In California, you can surf," I reminded her over by Artemis's mew.

She raised one dark eyebrow. "You can surf in Oregon, too. You just need a full wet suit."

I shrugged. "It's not the same."

"Yeah, here, the beach isn't full of towels and coolers and radios and people."

"Wouldn't know," I mumbled. "Never seen it."

"We'll have to get you over there."

"Water." Lucas walked up and tapped my chest with his index finger. "Don't get dehydrated. Leah, you want to learn how to give Artemis a shower?"

She beamed. "Absolutely."

He picked up a hose near his feet, turned it on to a low spray, and handed it to her. "Don't get too close to her mew. . . ."

Leah stood back and aimed the water through the wire. We heard rustling behind the blue tarp, and then the owl flew in a rush of wings to her perch. Drops gleamed on her feathers like diamonds. "She's so beautiful," Leah breathed.

I snorted. "She's mean."

A moth fluttered by. Instantly, Artemis's pupils filled her round eyes. Her feature tufts shot up. I stepped backward, knowing she couldn't fly through the mew's wire sides, but I was scared just the same. Lucas calmly retied his blond ponytail. "You know, kid, it's not really her fault. She's a human imprint. People made her the way she is; they failed her."

Failure. In my mind, I saw again the piece of paper wedged into my father's typewriter. I'd crumpled it into my trash can, but the word imprinted on my brain. Had I failed my father?

And if I had, would he ever come back to me?

CHAPTER ELEVEN
NOT A RETARD

Most families look pretty normal from the outside. Anyone looking at mine would see a father who works from home writing a book, a mother who does yoga and jogs while she looks for a new teaching job, and a kid who rides his bike all over town and helps to rehabilitate raptors.

But put my family under a magnifying glass and you'd see a really sad man who left his family and vanished, a mother gone silent and mean with worry, and a kid scared of owls. A kid who—every time he thought of his father—felt scared to death of death.

What would I see if I looked closer at Leah's family, at Lucas's, at Eric's?

Eric came to find me Saturday morning, a week after Dad took off. I sat in my room, staring out at the driveway, like if I just gazed at the potholed gravel long enough I could make the VW appear. I didn't see Eric until he tapped me on the shoulder.

"Don't surprise me like that!" I yelped.

His hair had a greenish tinge. He stood there in his bug T-shirt and denim shorts, grinning. "I dye it with Jeh-wo."

"*What?*"

"I dye my hair with Jeh-wo." His tongue danced in his mouth, trying to make me understand.

"Oh, *Jell-O*." I touched the ends of my hair. It was longer than I'd ever worn it, almost ponytail-length.

"I dye yours," Eric said. "Please, Solo?"

I turned away from the window. Dad said he'd come back. But he hadn't called, hadn't even written. Was he even alive?

"Okay. Let's go." I marched Eric past my mother's closed door and left without writing a note. Let Mom wonder if I'd run away, too.

In Mrs. Miller's kitchen, Eric poured hot water mixed with Jell-O powder into my hair. "Whoa! You purple, Solo."

I ran into his bathroom. My hair wasn't bright purple like the grapes on the Jell-O box, but just a little darker, sinister-looking.

"Why'd you dye your hair, Eric?" I scrubbed sticky streaks off my neck with one of his mom's washcloths.

Eric's thick fingers twisted his hair into spikes. "I be cool."

I couldn't help laughing. Eric would never be cool. His emotions lay right out there for everyone to see, like the bugs under his magnifying glass. Seriously *uncool*.

But I nodded at him just the same. "Your hair looks awesome, dude."

"What's going on here?" Mr. Miller loomed suddenly in the doorway, rasping his heavy, asthmatic breath. I hadn't seen him since the day he told the judge to throw me in jail. "Community service is too good for this kid!" he'd yelled.

I shrank behind the bathroom door and stared down at my purple-splotched feet.

"Solo and me have fun," Eric said. "See, Dad? I have green hair!"

Mr. Miller's eyes slid over him and shot bullets at me. He turned and stalked out the front door.

"Come on!" Eric ran out of the bathroom. We knelt on the couch and peered out the open window at his parents. They stood in the garden on opposite sides of Mrs. Miller's deer fence and glared at each other. Through the open window, we could hear every word they were saying.

"Why is that boy in my house?" Mr. Miller clenched his fists. His black three-piece suit and trench coat looked out of place surrounded by Mrs. Miller's corn and daisies and cheerful red tomatoes.

"He's Eric's friend!" Mrs. Miller whipped off her cowboy hat and shook it in his face. "Anyhow, what d'you care? You're never home."

"Someone's got to put food on the table."

"And someone's gotta make sure our son gets a chance at a normal life!"

"*Normal?*" Mr. Miller spat the word. "Our son will never be *normal*. He's a freak!"

I gripped Eric's arm. But he just sat there, staring through his magnifying glass. Did he not hear what his father had just said?

I looked back toward the window in time to see Mrs. Miller turn her back and Mr. Miller raise his fist. Slowly, she swiveled her head and looked at him over one shoulder.

She reminded me of this barn owl we had recently in the center's treatment room. The bird had been hit by a car, then mauled by a dog. It was so injured that Lucas could tube feed it without gloves and it didn't even try to shred his hand.

Mrs. Miller looked just like the owl—ready and waiting for more pain.

But Mr. Miller lowered his fist and stalked to his long black car.

"Goin' on another overnight business trip?" Mrs. Miller pulled her hat low over her eyes. Even from the living room, I saw tears shining on her cheeks as the car sped off. My throat stung.

"Solo? You hurt my arm." Eric pulled out of my grasp and rubbed the white marks I'd left on his sunburn. Then, matter-of-factly, he said, "My father hate me."

"He doesn't hate you," I said.

But I knew how he felt. Mine had left me, too.

"Hey, got any new bugs?" I jumped off the couch and headed for the stairs.

"I . . . I have a new spider. . . ."

"So show it to me!"

He followed me slowly up the stairs. We sat studying the spider's hairy legs through his magnifying glass when Mrs. Miller walked in. Her hands were muddy, and she had a big streak of dirt across one cheek, but her voice came out light, carefree.

"Wanna go downtown, partners? You can hang out in the arcade while I shop."

The arcade. I hadn't played video games since I'd sold mine at the yard sale.

"Cool!" Eric slapped me five.

I slapped him ten just to make him laugh. "I better call my mom, first," I said, picking up the phone's receiver.

I dialed the phone and listened to it ring. What if Dad picked up? I pictured how I'd drop the phone and sprint home on the dirt path through the forest—saw myself give him a huge hug and ask him go hiking up Spencer Butte. Then he'd see that there was no reason to drive away again.

"Hello?" Mom said into the phone, too quickly, so that I knew she'd been hoping for my father's voice instead of mine.

Words trembled on my tongue. "I'm . . . I'm going to the arcade with Eric."

"That's fine," she sighed. "Have fun."

"Call Mrs. Miller's cell phone if Dad comes home," I said super casual, like he'd just gone out for a gallon of milk. "Okay?"

"Okay. . . ." Mom echoed.

I hung up the phone.

On the way to the arcade, Mrs. Miller kept acting normal, like she wasn't married to the Lord of the Dark Side. But if you looked real close, you could see mascara smudged under her eye like a bruise. "How's your daddy?" she asked me.

My shoulders twitched. "Fine. He's . . . uh . . . he's off on a business trip for a couple days."

"Really? Where to?"

"Um . . . I'm not sure."

I looked out the window at the homeless people sitting near the fountain decorated with a school of metal salmon. Had he gone to join them? Or was he holed up in that expensive hotel right on the river, ordering room service and watching osprey go fishing in the river?

Wherever he went, why didn't he take me with him?

Mrs. Miller pulled the truck into the parking lot for the Down to Earth store and climbed out. "I've gotta find something to stop the deer, the slugs, and the cats from picnicking in my garden. Otherwise, we won't have corn on the cob for Eric's birthday next month. To which"—she kissed my head—"you are invited."

Eric clapped his hands. "I be fifteen!"

I resisted the urge to rub saliva out of my hair and took the stack of quarters Mrs. Miller handed me. "Thanks."

"Meetcha back here in one hour." She started to walk toward the garden store. Then she stopped and winked at me. "By the way, partners, nice hair."

Eric giggled and led me down the street toward the arcade. Right as we opened the door, two boys pushed past us—the same ones I'd seen at the canal the day Eric and I went fishing.

"Hey, look," said the one with the missing front tooth. "It's Killer and the retard! Nice magnifying glass, dingbat."

My heart began to flutter on nervous wings in my chest. "He's not a retard," I muttered. "Leave him alone."

The short kid with the bandana and the baseball cap stepped back, but Missing Tooth snarled like a mad dog. "Don't mess with us, trailer trash!"

The sun beat down, bouncing heat off the sidewalk. My hair felt sticky. A drop of sweat popped out on the back of my neck and crawled down my spine.

"Come in or shut the door!" A big guy waved a tattooed arm at us from behind the arcade counter. "You're letting the air conditioning out."

Missing Tooth wouldn't bother us with an adult around. "Let's go." I pulled Eric inside. The two kids followed us, then brushed by and headed for the back of the arcade.

"That boy is mean." Eric peered after Missing Tooth through his magnifying glass. Then he slapped a stack of quarters on the Final Fantasy game. "We do karate?"

Suddenly, I didn't feel like playing. I just didn't want to see dead people, even if they were pretend. "I'm gonna play Skee-Ball instead."

"Okey doke, Solo."

The Skee-Ball ramps stood off to the side, near an old Pac-Man game. I wandered over and dropped in two quarters. Heavy brown balls rolled toward me. I tossed them one at a time, aiming for the middle hole of the target—fifty points. The short kid with the bandana and the baseball cap walked up to the ramp right beside me. He dropped in coins, and balls rumbled out.

He's gonna crack me over the head with one.

He started rolling balls at his targets.

We each dropped in more quarters and played without talking. At last, he spoke up. "Heard you're working at that bird hospital."

He was baiting me, trying to start something. I ignored him and concentrated on rolling balls. One bounced into the 50 hole. Lightbulbs flashed on and off at the top of my ramp.

"Way to go."

I whipped around to face the kid. He shrugged. "No, seriously. You're pretty good."

He was awful—rolled the ball way too slow so it bounced into 10-point holes only.

"You have to roll it harder, like this." I curled my hand under the ball, swung my arm back, and let go. The ball rolled, caught air, and dropped into the 50 hole. Lightbulbs flashed again, and music jangled.

The kid tried to copy me. He swung his arm back and rolled. His ball took its sweet time wandering up the ramp, then dropped into the 20-point hole.

"Better." I looked sideways at him.

He tossed a ball up and caught it, then opened his mouth like he wanted to say something.

"Um . . ." He finally got the words out. "Sorry 'bout my friend. He's just fooling around."

I snorted. These days, I could spot a predator a mile away. Missing Tooth was out for blood. But this kid reminded me of Blinky—quiet, a little shy.

"Wanna go swimming at the river?" he asked. "I've got an inner tube. We could float down a couple miles, hike back up."

The river was nothing compared to the Pacific. No waves, no sand—just flat, boring water. But I missed swimming, feeling totally submerged like a fish. And it *was* hot.

"Maybe. Um . . . I'm Solo."

"I know. I'm Cody."

"How'd you know my name?"

"My dad's a cop in juvenile corrections, remember?"

All at once, the word *criminal* felt branded into my skin once more. I'd forgotten how it burned.

But Cody didn't seem to see it. "So you're from Southern Cal? Can you really walk around in shorts on Christmas?"

"We used to surf after we opened our presents."

"Cool!"

Missing Tooth swaggered up with a rope of licorice around his neck. "Look what I won, suckers."

"Hey." Cody socked him in the arm. "Solo's coming swimming with us."

"Whatever," Missing Tooth said with his mouth full. "What about *him*?"

We all looked at Eric. He'd used up his quarters, but he was still pretending to play Final Fantasy, pushing buttons and gnawing on his tongue.

Missing Tooth snickered. "We could walk right out the door and he wouldn't even notice."

Words formed in my head. *I'll be right back, Eric.* Or, *Do you wanna come swimming with us?* But they didn't come out.

"Where d'you swim?" I asked instead.

"We got a sweet spot . . . a secret." Missing Tooth narrowed his eyes. "But you gotta swear never to tell another soul. Not even your best friend, there."

"He's not my best friend. I swear."

We'd be gone just a few minutes, back before Eric even noticed. I started to tiptoe out behind them. Then I stopped.

I couldn't abandon him.

Eric turned to me. "Solo? You wanna play?"

Sweat trickled down his forehead, mixed with green Jell-O. Through his bangs, I saw the round, raised scar from where the shot had grazed him. My stomach went belly up.

Missing Tooth sneered. "Uh-oh. The retard's onto us."

I stared at a dried-up piece of gum on the dirty carpet. "I told you not to call him that."

Instantly, Missing Tooth was in my face. "You wanna fight, trailer trash?"

The man behind the counter raised his head from his newspaper, sensing trouble. Through his eyes, I saw how the movie might end.

```
FADE IN
EXTERIOR. ARCADE - DAY
```

Video games beeping and whistling, kids whooping. Suddenly, a handheld camera begins to bounce around the scene. People rush over, pointing and screaming at something.

CROWD (together)
Get him, Missing Tooth—kick that guy's butt. He's a criminal. Show him who's boss.

CLOSE-UP of blood spatters on the carpet.

PAN OUT to show a boy with long white hair pounding another boy's head into a pinball machine. A boy with Down syndrome looks on, hands helpless at his sides. The injured boy slumps to the carpet, his head gashed and bleeding.

> MISSING TOOTH
> That's for messing with me, trailer trash!
> Now I'm gonna waste your retard friend.

FADE OUT

"I don't want to fight," I mumbled to the boys in front of me.

Cody shrugged and walked toward the door. "Leave 'em alone. It's too hot."

But there was no stopping Missing Tooth. "How 'bout you?" He stuck his face close to Eric's. "You wanna fight, retard?"

What happened next shocked me more than if a hawk had swooped into the arcade, grabbed the dried-up piece of gum beside my shoe, and started blowing pink bubbles.

"I *not* a retard!" Eric yelled.

Then he karate-kicked Missing Tooth, Final Fantasy style, right in the jaw.

CHAPTER TWELVE
NICTITATING MEMBRANES

Eric and I didn't tell Mrs. Miller what had happened in the arcade, how Missing Tooth held his jaw like his teeth might fall out, sputtering blood and spitting curses until Cody pulled him out the door and they disappeared down the street. How the man behind the counter saw the whole thing and only flashed this little grin at Eric before he went back to talking on the cell phone in his hand.

"Nice move, Eric," I said when his mother went into Subway for sandwiches and chips.

He grinned. "I get a black belt in karate."

We ate in a park with little kids who swarmed like ants around an ice cream truck that blared carnival music in the parking lot. Mrs. Miller bought us Popsicles to eat in the truck on the way home. She let me out in front of the trailer. The Big Grape's parking spot still stood empty. "When's your daddy get back?" she asked.

I bit my lip. "Soon."

"Come on over tomorrow if you want to help Eric and me make berry tarts. We'll start early, before things heat up outside."

"Okay. Thanks for the sandwich and Popsicle. Bye, Eric."

They left, and I climbed the porch steps, dread slowing my feet. Inside the trailer, bluish smoke drifted down the hallway like car exhaust.

Mom's dead.

I sprinted down the hall and burst through my parents' bedroom door. My mother sat cross-legged on the carpet surrounded by flickering candles. Her thumbs and index fingers made circles on her knees. At the sound of my gasp, her eyes flew open. "What's wrong, Solo?"

I coughed to hide the terror that had yanked me down the hall. "Geez. What's with the smoke?"

"I'm burning sage." She sucked in a long breath through her nostrils. "My yoga teacher says it helps ward off evil spirits."

"*Evil spirits?*"

"I'm meditating, Solo."

"Why?"

My mother blinked, reminding me of Hermes at the raptor center. Owls have *nictitating membranes*—second eyelids that sweep across their eyes, windshield wiper–style—to protect them from injuries when they get into it with a rodent or smaller bird. Mom's eyes looked blurry, as if she had nictitating membranes, too.

What were they protecting her from? Me?

She sighed and stretched her legs out in front of her, folded her arms tight across her chest. "I'm *trying* to calm my mind and reach out to your father. Wherever he is, maybe he'll sense how much we love him and come back to us."

"*If* he's still alive." I couldn't stop the words from bursting out. I wanted her to get angry, to order me to stop all the drama and look on the bright side of life, to walk on the sunny side of the street, and to never give up hope . . . every cliché in the book.

Instead, she dropped her head to her chest. "If he's still alive," she echoed in a tiny voice.

I didn't cry. Just slammed the screen door, grabbed my bike, and ran up the hill until my lungs begged for air. At the top, I climbed on and flew down the hill. I rode hard into town and skidded to a stop in front of the library. Wherever Dad was, maybe he'd check his email.

I loped up the round staircase to the second floor and the computers, logged onto the Internet with my new library card, and sent a message to my father's Gmail address:

Dad,
How are you? I'm OK. Mom's OK, too. I miss you.
Will you come back soon?

Love, Solo

I sent it. Biked home and waited. But he didn't come back on Sunday. And he didn't email me back. Sunday afternoon, I biked back to the library and stayed until it closed, checking my email every five minutes. Instead, finally, there was a note from Blinky.

Solo—

You back? My mom thinks she saw your dad at the DMV. Rajen and Eldon say hi.

My fingers pounded the keyboard, shooting back a message to my friend.

In the California DMV?

I raced home. Mom knelt in her garden, planting some poor seedlings from a plastic six-pack into hot soil. I left my bike against the trailer and tiptoed in, grabbing her phone to call my grandma.

"Hey, Gram." I kept my voice low, not wanting Mom to hear and get her hopes up. "It's Solo. Is my dad there?"

Her voice sounded confused. "Why would he be *here*, honey? Isn't he with you?"

My mother appeared in the kitchen doorway. The corners of her mouth turned down, and she wiped one hand across her eyes, leaving a big streak of garden dirt. "I already called her."

"Oh." I looked away toward the spiderweb stretched across a corner of the kitchen window. A fly hung there, lifeless. "Sorry, Gram. He must be at the store. Thanks."

I hung up before she could ask me any more questions, then walked slowly down the hall. I held my breath against the sickly sweet scent of incense wafting out of Mom's bedroom—it was worse than any smell the raptor center offered.

Exhausted, I crawled into bed. It was only eight o'clock. The summer sun had just begun to set behind the trees. I fell asleep in a strip of orange-gold light that slipped in between the curtains and didn't wake up for twelve hours.

•

The next morning, I rode into town to check my email before my shift at the raptor center. But as I flew down the hill, something hissed behind me. *Rattlesnake?*

I glanced behind me. My back tire splayed out floppy against the rim. I rolled the Pig Wheel off the road and flipped it upside down. I glanced at my watch. Nine forty. My shift started at ten. I kicked a rock across the road.

It took me fifteen minutes to patch my bike tube the way Sergeant Bird Nerd had showed me, with a patch kit and tire levers and a tube of stinky glue. Not even a green-shirter from the Tour de France could make it to the raptor center in five minutes.

I pedaled hard into town and raced toward Eyrie Road. Sweat poured into my eyes, burning them so that I had to squint against the sting. I jammed my sneakers into my toe clips and dropped the bike into the smallest gear. My pedals spun up the steep driveway.

Minerva met me outside the clinic, pale fists dug into her skinny hips. "You're late!" she snapped. "Next time, call and let me know. I'd hate to have to report you to your social worker."

I stared at her in her stupid owl shirt. My shirt dripped with sweat and my legs shook like saplings on a windy day. Before I could say something I might regret, Lucas walked out of the office and socked me in the shoulder.

"Flat tire?" He raised his eyebrow at my black, greasy hands.

"Took a while to change," I muttered.

"First time's the hardest."

Minerva didn't seem to hear us. She kept barking orders like a prison warden. "I want you two to clean the mews really well. I found algae in Xerxes's water tub." She glared at me. "Solo, I noticed you're not feeding the great horned owl in the treatment room like I asked you to. From now on, Lucas will feed him."

"Fine. It's not like I . . ."

Lucas shot me a warning look that silenced me.

"You can feed the cat in the office bathroom. You won't see her—she's feral. Give her a bowlful of crunchies and change her water." Minerva slammed the door behind her and stalked off to her apartment.

"*She's* feral," Lucas whispered.

I poured water from my bike bottle over my head. "What d'you mean, feral?"

"Wild," he said. "Scared and mean."

"She *is* mean." I bent down to scrub bike grease off my leg.

"Don't worry, kid. She'll forget about it in a couple days, and you can go back to feeding the birds."

"She can feed her own stupid birds!"

Sergeant Bird Nerd snapped to attention. "You're here for the birds. Remember that." He lowered his voice. "Better feed that cat before she comes out again."

"I'm not here to help *cats*." I stomped into the clinic and threw down my backpack. From his mew, Hermes clacked his beak and leapt onto his pink tennis shoe. "I'm not here for you, either," I muttered and stalked to the bathroom.

The bathroom next to the clinic was small, just big enough for a microscope, a toilet, and a sink full of empty syringes. There weren't many hiding places. Still, I couldn't find the cat. I dumped food into an empty cream cheese container and looked around.

Nothing.

At last, I heard her. "*Prrrpt?*"

The sound came from behind the trash can. I got down on all fours and glimpsed the tip of a black tail, crooked as a bent finger.

"I think she's got a broken tail," Lucas called from the treatment room.

"No kidding."

Carefully, I lifted the can away from the wall. A black and white blur shot by me and disappeared into the clinic. This was no cat. It was a kitten the size of my hand, a ball of long-haired fluff covered in mats and burrs. *I could take her home*, I thought, *clean her up, make her mine*.

Then, I remembered the owl.

"People drop stray cats at the bottom of the driveway," he explained, "thinking if we rescue birds, we'll rescue other animals, too. Some of them find their way up here. She let me pick her up, but she hates being inside."

He stretched out his arm raked with red scratches that crisscrossed the three parallel white scars near his wrist.

Hermes was going bonkers in his mew, dancing around and craning his neck to see where the kitten had hidden herself. Lucas found her and fished her out from behind the desk by the loose scruff of her neck. She yowled. He wrapped her in a towel and plunged a syringe of water into her mouth. "She's dehydrated."

"That makes two of us." I downed a mug of water and turned away while he put the kitten back into the bathroom. I didn't want to look at her—it hurt too much.

"Look, kid. Let me feed the birds in the treatment room this one time, just to pacify Minerva. Then we can clean enclosures."

"Dude, I don't *want* to feed the birds in the treatment room. I'm glad she took me off that job."

"Solo, I want you to water all the flowers." Minerva pushed through the screen door, red hair on top of her head in a sloppy bun and a wet towel around her sunburned neck. "Today's gonna be a scorcher."

I knocked my water bottle into the sink. It rattled around, and Hermes shot into a narrow brown arrow. He let out a surprised hoot.

"Quiet!" Minerva snapped. "We've got birds recuperating in here."

"Can I ask you something about the red-tail's medication?" Lucas stepped between Minerva and me. I bolted out of the office and unrolled the long green hose.

"I'm not a gardener." I fumed.

Pots of flowers hung from the visitor's center and the office. I splashed in water, slopping soil over the sides. Then I yanked the hose up the hill and shot a hard stream of water toward the butterfly garden.

WHOO-hoo-oo-oo-oo-WHOO-WHOO!

Artemis called to me, already on her perch.

"Go away. I don't have time for you."

The owl spread out her wings and waited. I kept watering flowers. She called again, and the white feathers on her breast fluttered. Lucas said those feathers helped owls to recognize each other across a dark forest.

Did Artemis recognize me?

153

"Fine. It's not like I have anything better to do." I turned the hose on her.

She tilted one wing down and closed her eyes halfway. Water drops beaded on black and brown striped feathers. I studied the yellow irises, her curved black talons gripping the perch. "Minerva better keep that kitten away from you."

"Don't worry—I will."

I hated the way Minerva always showed up beside me, like she'd been beamed from hyperspace. She stood there smiling at me, like we hadn't just gone fifteen rounds together before she knocked me on my butt.

"Would you like to go with Lucas to the coast on Saturday? He's releasing the great horned owl from the treatment room . . . the one you helped to rehabilitate."

I looked sideways at her. "My shift's Monday through Friday, remember?"

"Something bothering you, Solo? You seem edgy today."

"So do you!"

I bit the words back too late. My community service was supposed to last another two weeks. If Minerva fired me from the raptor center, would I have to go to jail?

She only nodded. "You're right. I *am* edgy. I lost a bird today."

"Lost a bird?" I scanned the cloudless blue sky, peered into the tops of the firs. "Where is it?"

She didn't answer.

"You mean . . . it *died?*"

She pressed her knuckles against her lips. "One of the red-tailed hawks. She contracted a virus. . . ."

I whipped around to stare at the hawk mew. Only one bird sat on the perch, head drooping. They'd liked to sit side by side, sun gleaming on their red-feathered tails.

"I'm . . . uh . . . really sorry."

Now I understood why people apologized after a loss. When someone dies, there's nothing else to say.

"Death sucks," I mumbled.

Why was my father so obsessed with it?

Minerva folded her arms across her chest. "If you're going to participate in life, to fight for it, you've got to renegotiate death every day. I know that. But to lose a hawk today . . . on the anniversary of my mother's . . ." Her voice trailed off, and she looked past Artemis at something I couldn't see.

"I used to be a white-water rafting guide in Alaska. My mother came up to visit . . . she drowned on a river run. Not my fault; she was in someone else's boat, and it hit a hole. . . ."

Her throat bobbed, and she closed her eyes. "That evening, I saw a snowy owl on my cabin roof. They're magnificent birds—huge and pure white. I guess you could say that night was my *kriyā*."

"Cry-a?"

"It's a Sanskrit word." She reached for the hose and began to shower Artemis. "Means 'spiritual emergency' or 'surrender.' I gave up everything that day. My mother, my job, my home. A week later, I moved here and started a new life."

My father's gone.

I wanted to tell her, but I couldn't say the words out loud. That would make them true.

"It's funny," Minerva continued. "After a while, I stopped thinking about myself and focused on the birds . . . then, I began to heal."

I thought of the bumper sticker on her car. FOLLOW YOUR BLISS.

"What if Alaska was your bliss?" I asked her.

She nodded. "Thankfully, I think we're granted more than one bliss."

The phone jangled from the office. "Can you get that? I sent Lucas to the vet's office."

I ran down the path and picked up the phone. Leah.

"Hey there, Solo," she said in her high-pitched voice. "Is Minerva around?"

"She's up with Artemis."

I looked down at a note on the desk and recognized Lucas's chicken scratch.

Solo—

I'm releasing an owl at the coast Saturday. Want to come? Pick you up at your house, 3:00. Call me.

Lucas

Next to the note, he'd drawn a sketch of a great horned owl. A decent sketch.

"I'll leave Minerva a message that you called," I told Leah.

"Thanks. Hey, everything okay? You sound weird."

Minerva said she felt better after she stopped thinking about her own problems and focused on helping someone else. But I was just a kid. What could I do to help anyone?

Suddenly, I knew. I thought of all those movies Dad had made me watch—screwball comedies, he called them—where Katherine Hepburn and Cary Grant or Myrna Loy and William Powell argued and joked and finally fell in love. If I could write a screwball comedy on paper, why couldn't I direct a real-life romance?

"Um . . . Leah?" I stammered, thinking hard as I spoke. "Lucas wanted me to tell you we're releasing that great horned owl at the coast tomorrow. Be at my house by three in the afternoon if you want to go."

I gave her my address. I'd make sure to meet her by the mailbox, so she wouldn't see the trailer.

She laughed. "Awesome! That sounds like fun. See you tomorrow, then!"

Lucas would be so excited when he saw Leah the next day all ready to go on a road trip with us. In spite of the fear that banged itself against the sides of my brain like a crazy caged bird, the thought of Sergeant Bird Nerd happy actually made me smile.

Chapter Thirteen
JUST LET GO

I'm going to the coast to release a great horned owl."
My mother looked up from the laptop she'd borrowed
from Mrs. Miller to conduct her endless sleuthing
for my father.

"With *whom* are you driving an *hour* to the coast?
Shouldn't you have *asked* me first?"

I couldn't afford to make her mad. "I'm going with
Sergeant . . . with Lucas from the raptor center."

"He's an adult?"

"He's twenty-five. He works with at-risk youth." I
choked a little over the words.

Mom closed the laptop and studied me. Since I'd
finally pulled the bandages off my arm, two raised white
scars were the only evidence that I'd been gashed by a
giant bird.

"Why do you want to go, Solo?" she asked me. "I
thought you *hated* birds, and the center, too."

I stood there with my jaw hanging down, but the words wouldn't come out.

Because I'm sick of thinking about myself.

Because I'm sick of worrying that you might go even crazier.

Because I'm sick of worrying that Dad might be dead.

A knock on the door saved me from answering her.

"Dad?" I yelped without thinking.

But why would my father knock on his own door?

Leah.

I raced to the front door, combing my hair with my fingers. But Eric, not Leah, stood on the porch. He held out a book in one hand and a fuzzy black and orange caterpillar in the other.

I scowled. "What are you doing here?"

"We catch bugs today?"

"Sorry. I'm releasing an owl at the coast today."

"Where on the coast?"

I wasn't sure, exactly. "It's where a lot of owls live. Go home, okay? I'll catch up with you later."

Leah didn't need to see me hanging around Eric with his giant magnifying glass and his pink butterfly T-shirt.

But Eric stood rooted to the porch. He held up the book. "My father come home last night. He bring me this bug book."

To make up for calling his son a freak.

I peered down the empty driveway, then reached for the book. "Lemme see." I flipped through the pictures of beetles and centipedes. "Cool. I gotta go."

I turned to my mother. She'd reopened the laptop, but just slumped at her chair, staring into space. "Bye, Mom. *Mom?*"

Startled by my voice, she sat up. "Sorry. Be careful. Need some money?"

I grabbed my backpack and the crumpled five-dollar bill she fished out of her purse. "Thanks, Mom. Bye."

Eric trotted down the driveway after me. "Who that girl?"

He pointed at Leah, who was walking up the driveway with her silver road bike. No way had she missed the tin can trailer. Maybe I could convince her it was Eric's.

"Do you live here, Solo?" She tugged down the brim of her Dodgers cap. "That's so cool! I've always wanted a trailer on some land. You off the grid?"

"Off the what?"

"Do you get your electricity from solar power?"

"I don't think so."

"You could if you put solar cells on top of it."

Eric stuck his hand out toward Leah. "I Eric Miller. Solo my friend."

"I'm not his . . . he's my neighbor," I stammered. But Leah shook Eric's hand and looked into his eyes like maybe lots of her friends had Down syndrome.

"Nice to meet you, Eric. Coming with us?"

His grin nearly split his face in two. "I am, Solo?"

Then Leah turned the full force of her smile on me. Serious solar power.

"Oh, fine." I shrugged. "Go make sure your mom says it's okay."

"Hold my caterpillar!" Eric dropped the fuzzy black and orange caterpillar into my hand and trotted down the path to his house.

Leah laughed. "I can tell you're a great friend, Solo."

I stood there speechless with a bug crawling around in my hand.

"Nice of Lucas to let me come along," she said then. "I didn't think he liked me much."

"Yeah." I remembered my plan from the day before— to direct a real-life romantic comedy. "Sergeant Bird Nerd's pretty cool."

But when Lucas drove up and saw Leah standing by the mailbox, he looked anything but cool. He almost ran her over.

"Good afternoon," he enunciated, getting out of his truck. The way his eyebrows thundered over his nose, I knew it wasn't a good afternoon at all. He wore a ratty blue sweater that looked like a bird had nested in it, and his bandana was crooked. Real quick, he straightened it and smoothed down his blond ponytail. His eyes fired a question into mine. *What's* she *doing here?*

"Leah's gonna help us," I said before he could give me grief.

The eyebrows leapt into his hairline. I looked away. Why had I thought this would work? He hated girls. And now, he hated me.

Mrs. Miller rumbled up in her truck. Eric jumped out with a huge backpack and his magnifying glass around his neck. "My mother say I go!"

Lucas looked from me to Leah. "Who's *this*?"

Eric stuck out his hand. "I Eric Miller."

"Howdy," Mrs. Miller called out the window. "So, you run the raptor center."

He shook his head. "I'm just a volunteer. We all are."

"Well, it's awful nice of you to invite Eric to the coast to release that owl."

"Uh . . . well . . . no problem," Lucas said. Did she hear the annoyance in his voice, too?

I dropped Eric's caterpillar on a nearby bush and yanked him into the back of the truck before Lucas could reconsider. "We'll keep an eye on the bird," I called and jumped inside.

The owl shifted in its pet carrier, covered with a sheet. Lucas walked over to close the tailgate. "Why's *she* here?" he hissed at me.

I squirmed like one of the mealworms he fed to Hermes. "We needed help. It's a big bird, and I'm a short kid."

Lucas looked down his hawk nose at me. He looked about as far from a romantic hero as I looked from a surfer in my hiking boots and wide-brimmed hat.

"You've got it all thought out, don't you, kid?" He slammed the tailgate closed and started the truck. Was it my imagination, or did he take off extra fast, lurching

163

into gear so Eric and I fell forward and thwacked our heads against the seat? Under the sheet, the owl clacked its beak.

"Relax, Eric." I nudged his chubby legs with my sneaker. "He won't bite."

"I not worried. This is fun!"

The truck bed had narrow, tinted windows. Up ahead, I could just make out two kids at the bus stop. Cody and Missing Tooth.

Eric saw them, too. "I kick that guy's butt!" he giggled.

I couldn't help it. I laughed. "You sure did." I slid open the window.

Then, amazingly, Eric read my mind. Together, we yelled the same thing: "*I not a retard!*"

Missing Tooth stared at the truck and opened his mouth to yell, but Lucas sped off before he could make a sound.

After that, the day got better. I leaned against the pet carrier and studied Lucas and Leah through the little open window separating the truck bed from the cab. It reminded me of a movie frame. My screen-writing teacher had told us that if we wanted to study the way real people talk, we should eavesdrop when-ever possible.

I pulled out my notebook and scribbled down as much as I could of the conversation in front of me. Nothing Oscar-winning, but it got better the longer we drove.

JUST LET GO

FADE IN
INTERIOR. TRUCK - DAY

LUCAS and LEAH sit on opposite sides of
the long bench seat, silent as hawks. His
back is sergeant-stiff, and he grips the
steering wheel with both hands. She leans
against the door, looking out the window.
Finally, she turns to him with her eyes
blue as the summer sky.

> LEAH
> Thanks for asking me along on the
> trip. I'm writing a report on raptor
> rehabilitation for my environmental
> studies class.

> LUCAS
> (like he's a professor)
> Owls are fascinating. They're at the
> top of the food chain, so we can
> study them to see the effects of pes-
> ticides and environmental changes.

Leah nods. Then she reaches into her backpack and pulls out a paper bag.

                    LEAH
Want a cookie? They're chocolate
chip. I just baked them this morning.

Lucas bites into the cookie she hands
him. Suddenly, he smiles.

                    LUCAS
I'm impressed. You know how to hold
owls *and* bake cookies. Um . . . can
I have another one?

"What'cha writing, Solo?" Leah interrupted my screenplay and pushed a handful of cookies through the window. Oatmeal chocolate chip, still warm. "You guys okay back there?"

Eric popped a cookie into his mouth. "Smells like trash," he said, spraying crumbs.

My stomach lurched. The truck bed did smell like garbage—raptor center garbage. It pretty much killed my appetite.

"Hey, Lucas. Don't you wash this thing after you dump the trash?" I called through the window.

Lucas glanced at me over his shoulder. "Why, I'm sorry, Solo. I didn't realize you'd be riding in the back this afternoon. Otherwise, I would have hung up an air freshener."

The truck rounded a corner. Fir-covered mountains spread out before us. In the middle of all that green stood one lone hill, bald and brown.

Lucas shook his head. "Wow. Two weeks ago, that was covered with trees. Betcha some landowner's just made a fortune clear-cutting it and selling the lumber."

Rajen used to get a kick out of pretending he was a Buddhist monk. It was when we were studying haiku—Bashō and Issa and those guys—in class. He'd sit cross-legged and sober up his face, eyes half-lidded. "If a tree falls in a forest and no one is around," he'd intone, "does it make a sound?"

Stupid question. There's always someone in the forest, someone listening when a tree falls.

The bare mountain depressed me. I turned to Eric. "Hey, know what kind of raptors live in those Douglas firs?"

He barely heard me. His eyes stayed fixed on Leah, a big grin on his face. "She pretty," he said.

"Dude." I shook my head. "She's in *college*. Way too old for you."

He shrugged. "I love that girl."

I understood. I guess I sort of loved her in a way, even though I knew it was impossible. Maybe Lucas was beginning to love her a little, too.

"Hey." Lucas stretched his right arm across the top of the bench seat. "Did you hear about the woman who lived in a tree for two years to protest logging?"

Leah bounced in her seat, eyes wide and excited. "Yeah! Wasn't there a guy who sat in a tree downtown for a month?"

Now they were off, chattering about people who lived in trees, slept in trees, and chained themselves to trees to keep loggers from chopping down forests.

Eric gave up staring at Leah and turned to the pet carrier. He lifted one corner of the sheet. The great horned owl huddled in one corner, a trembling pile of brown and black feathers. He hissed when he saw us.

"I wouldn't feel too sorry for him," I told Eric.

•

After an hour, Lucas slowed his truck to make a left turn. For a while, we followed a river bluer than the one that ran through our city. I showed Eric a big osprey nest on a piece of plywood nailed to a long post. "They're fishing birds," I told him. "Big black and white guys who swoop down and grab trout in their talons."

The air cooled, and I smelled something familiar . . . kelp and saltwater.

"Here we are!" Lucas called. I followed his finger to the long line of blue stretched out between sand dunes. *The ocean.*

Eric held up his magnifying glass. "I see sharks!"

"You can't see sharks from the land. . ." I began, then gave up. "Are we getting out soon?"

I had to see those waves.

"Soon." Lucas drove a while longer, then pulled into a parking lot. He hopped out of the cab and swung open the tailgate. "How's our owl?"

"Scared." I jumped out, sucking in salty air. Pines bent into weird shapes stood around us, hiding the ocean from view.

"We have to hike a little ways to get to where they found the owl." Lucas opened the passenger door for Leah.

Eric jumped to the ground, shouldered his mammoth backpack, and walked over to her. "I have more cookies?"

She shook the paper bag, giggling. "Lucas ate them all."

Now Sergeant Bird Nerd was all business. "Let's get the owl out of the hot truck. We don't want to release him all dehydrated."

He lifted the pet carrier. We walked after him past the parking lot to a sandy path and followed it to a pond, dark water surrounded by more crooked pines. The owl rustled and screeched. He knew he was home. But when we got to the pond, instead of just setting down the pet carrier and letting him go, Lucas decided to make a speech.

"Two kids found this owl here." He put the carrier on a tree stump and straightened his bandana over his ponytail. "The owl flew into a power line and got electrocuted, then fell to the ground and got tangled up in fishing line. He should have died, but he's strong—proof that no matter what life throws at us, we can survive."

Leah reached out and touched his ratty sweater sleeve. Lucas cleared his throat and met my eyes. "Thanks to us, this owl is ready to fly free."

"Fly!" Eric cried.

Leah knelt and pulled the sheet off the carrier. The owl stared out from between the bars, yellow eyes locked on the trees. Lucas pulled on his leather gloves and tossed me a pair from his backpack. "Here, kid."

"What're these for?"

"You get to release him."

"Me?" I jumped back. "Uh . . ."

Lucas pinned me with his eyes. "You."

Me. I pulled the gloves over my hands, heart thwacking in my ears. Lucas reached into the carrier and scooped up the owl. The bird's feathered toes looked enormous. Each black talon had its own little sword, and his hooked beak was another. Nine weapons on one bird. Was the owl a murderer, or was he just trying to survive . . . like me?

"Take him." Lucas held out the owl. "Grab his legs in your hands and hold him tight against you, so he doesn't hurt his wings."

I reached out.

In *Star Wars*, Obi-Wan Kenobi and Darth Vader fight a lightsaber showdown—good against evil—in white and black robes. At last, Vader strikes a death blow. Then, all that's left of his enemy is an empty brown robe, almost weightless.

The owl felt so light in my hands. Even through the gloves, I could tell he was mostly feathers. He weighed two pounds, maybe three. His fluffy head tufts jutted inches from my face. Good and evil battled in my gut. The owl clacked his beak.

"Throw him into the air," Lucas told me.

"I don't wanna hurt him. . . ."

"You won't. Trust me."

Leah bent close to my ear, whispered, "Just let go."

I took a deep breath and tossed the owl toward the sky. Instantly, his wings stretched out and he sailed across the pond into a pine tree.

And then, all that was left of my anger was a memory, which was almost weightless.

Chapter Fourteen
NO LONGER A BUTTE

Congratulations!" Leah hugged me. Her hair smelled like vanilla. Suddenly, I felt light, like I could fly up into the trees with the owl.

Lucas threw an arm around my shoulders, weighing me down. "Way to go, kid."

"Yay, Solo!" Eric hugged me too and almost knocked us all over. We stood together in the sand, watching the owl. He sat on a branch and peered out at the trees and the pond like he couldn't believe his eyes.

"Welcome home!" Eric looked through his magnifying glass at the bird.

"Here." Lucas offered his binoculars. "Now you can have owl vision."

Our guy wasn't doing much—just meditating up in his tree. And then, without warning, he spread his wings and flew across an open place in the pines, vanishing into the forest. "He'll stay there until dinnertime," Lucas told us.

Mice lived in that forest, and rabbits, and squirrels, and chipmunks. I heard Minerva's voice. *Life feeds on life. Get used to it.*

Leah pointed to a sandy path near the pond. "That leads to the ocean. Do we have time for a hike?"

Lucas pointed at me. "Solo, your eyes are bigger than the owl's. Go!"

I took off running down the sandy trail. Eric panted behind me, weighed down by his enormous backpack. "Wait, Solo!"

But I couldn't wait. The ocean called to me. My feet flew, slipping and sliding over sand dunes, racing through pine trees to the edge of a low, sandy cliff.

The beach stretched out empty and white. No people anywhere. Huge rocks stuck up from the water, and waves crashed turquoise onto the shore. I kicked off my sandals and scooted down the cliff side to the beach and ran straight into the water. The ocean foamed cold around my ankles.

Welcome back.

I splashed out and ducked under, swallowing a mouthful of saltwater. It stung my throat, bitter and familiar. I surfaced and swam toward seagulls bobbing beyond the breakers. Oregon's ocean felt colder, way colder, than California's piece of the Pacific. I floated on my back, shivering, and gazed at the forest bordering the beach, dark green against impossible blue.

Eric stood at the shoreline. Lucas hovered farther back on the beach. I didn't see Leah anywhere. Then, a wet head popped up beside me. She giggled through chattering teeth. "It's freezing!" Her cheeks glowed pink. "Here comes a wave. Let's catch it!"

Side by side, we caught the wave and bodysurfed. "Go, Ducks!" Leah cried.

"Ducks?" I panted.

"The university's mascot. You've gotta come with me to a football game sometime!"

From the shore, Lucas yelled at us to come in. He stood beside Eric, both of them waving their arms like crazy.

"He's scared we'll get hypothermia." Leah smiled, her lips tinged blue. "We'd better go in."

"He's being ri . . . ri . . . ridiculous!" My own teeth chattered hard.

"Maybe not. My fingers are going numb."

That's when I noticed mine were numb, too. "Race you in!"

We swam hard toward shore. A wave glided up and I rode it in, landing almost at Lucas's sneakers. Leah bodysurfed just behind me.

Lucas tossed me my sandals. "You caught that wave like a pro."

"I learned to surf when I was four."

He dropped his ratty sweater over Leah's shoulders. She left the thing on, even thanked him for it. We collapsed on the sand and watched Eric stalk a flock of black-beaked birds skittering back and forth on the shoreline. A weird, creaky sound came from beside me.

"My stomach." Lucas's face flushed. "Forgot to eat breakfast . . . and lunch."

My appetite had vanished after Dad left. But now I felt it gnawing around the edges of my hollow gut.

"I'm thirsty." Leah looked back at the trail. "I left my water bottle in the car."

Eric reached for his huge backpack. "I have food!"

"No way!"

He pulled out a plastic bag full of Mrs. Miller's peanut butter and banana sandwiches. A green canteen of water came next, then apples, and finally, a package of Oreos.

"Woo-hoo!"

We slapped each other five, and Leah hugged Eric. "You're awesome!"

A slow pink flush stained Eric's cheeks. "I give you *all* the cookies." He handed her the package, and she giggled. Lucas kicked back on the sand, watching them with the corners of his mouth twisted up.

I wondered what he was thinking. With her hair all wet and saltwater drying like crystals on her legs, Leah looked like a mermaid. He must've noticed.

I hoped Leah was thinking about Lucas.

Eric was thinking about Leah—I knew it.

And me?

I wasn't thinking about Mom. I wasn't even wondering if Dad would return. I stretched out in the golden sunlight, one thought in my head: *I have friends—good ones. I'm no longer a butte.*

"Why d'you and Lucas carry notebooks in your pocket?" Leah tossed a crust of bread toward the shore birds. "Is it something to do with the raptor center?"

Lucas and I blinked at each other. He pulled his notebook out of his back pocket and opened it.

"*You* did these drawings?" Leah's eyes widened at the penciled hawks and owls.

Lucas ducked his head. "They're just sketches. They're not any good."

"They're fantastic! Are you an artist, too, Solo?"

I'd forgotten about the notebook in the pocket of my shorts. I pulled it out. Waterlogged, the pages stuck to each other and shredded as I tried to turn them. "I'm a writer." I stared down at the wad of ruined scenes.

"We could iron them."

"No point." My words had faded and blurred, unreadable. I shoved the pages into my soaked pocket. "I'll write more."

She handed me another half of a sandwich. "I'd love to read your work."

Lucas stood up, squinted at the sun. "We'd better head back. It's a long way back to the city."

This time, we all rode in the truck cab—Lucas driving, Leah squashed next to him, me on her other side, and Eric pressed against the door. "This is extremely illegal." Lucas caught my eye and shrugged. "But it's better than smelling like garbage."

I grinned. "Next time I ride in your truck, I'll bring my gas mask."

We dropped Eric off at his house, and Mrs. Miller waved to us from her garden. "Thank you," she called. "Hope the sandwiches came in handy."

"They sure did, Mrs. M.!" I called back.

I was next. "You can let me off at the mailboxes," I told Lucas.

He shook his head. "No way. I want to see your place, kid." His truck rumbled up the gravel driveway and he let out a whistle. "That's a sweet VW."

My eyes bugged out. There in the driveway stood The Big Grape.

Dad.

"Thanks, Lucas. See you Monday, Leah."

I leapt out of the truck and ran toward the trailer, yelling. "Dad? Hey, Dad?"

He met me at the door. His arms went around me, and he squashed me against his chest. "I'm so, so sorry, Solo," he said. "I had to go." He pulled back and looked into my face. "I got a lot of things straightened out in my head. And I made a decision."

Over his shoulder, I saw my mother sitting at the table with her hands folded, her face inscrutable.

Are they getting a divorce?

Is he leaving us for good?

"Son," my father said, "we're moving back to California."

CHAPTER FIFTEEN
PARENTS = CHAOS

Up until my father tried to commit suicide, I had a good life. I went to school, surfed, played video games, hung out with my friends, and wrote screenplay scenes. It's hard to see what's missing from your life if you haven't lived it yet. I hated Dad for being depressed, hated Mom for making us change everything.

How could I have known the change would be good?

I couldn't point to the moment my new life began to mean freedom instead of prison. Maybe it was the day I hiked to the top of Spencer Butte and got a wide-angle view of the world. Maybe it was the afternoon I met Lucas or Leah, or even Eric. Maybe it happened the instant I released the great horned owl in the forest.

All I knew for sure was that Dad's words should have made me rush to my room and start packing for migration down south. Instead, the words lodged in my chest like an indigestible rat bone.

"Moving?" I choked.

Dad's eyes filled with tears. "We robbed you of a wonderful life, son. You had everything . . ."

He pressed his fingers against his eyelids. "I drove down to Los Angeles to meet with my old boss. He said I can have my job back. . . ."

I glared at him. "I thought you were gonna write a book."

He sighed. "It's not that easy, Solo. *You* can fill page after page in those notebooks of yours. And it's good stuff." He shrugged at my surprised look. "I've read your scenes. You're a born writer."

"So are you!" I shot back.

"We've got to return to California," Dad said. "We tried an experiment, and it failed."

"You didn't give it a chance! You never even went outside!"

Beside me, my mother inhaled one of her deep yoga breaths. She stood and exhaled loudly, put her hands on my shoulders. "Don't you *want* to move back, Solo?"

She waited a long time for my answer. Everything around me waited, too. The cicadas stopped chirping in the yard. The frogs down by the pond stopped croaking. Even the hawk on the telephone pole sat motionless. Finally, I spoke.

"I don't know."

For just a moment, I saw Rajen and Blinky and me together again, striding down the beach with our surfboards. Maybe I could even be friends with Eldon. But sooner or later, I'd head out for the deep water where the biggest waves broke, alone. Then I'd remember.

Impossibly tall trees. The caw of crows and the hooting of owls. Lucas nailing perches together, smoothing down his crazy ponytail. Leah misting diamonds of water onto Artemis's feathers.

I glared at my father. Then, I let go the words I'd been holding onto ever since he'd tried to commit suicide, all those months ago.

"I hate you."

I stumbled blindly down the hall and into my room.

I didn't know what I was going to do until I was doing it. I kicked off my wet sandals, laced up Mom's thrift store hiking boots, and balled up a jacket. I wrapped the Darth Vader bank in a blanket, muffling the jangle of falling coins as they fell into my backpack. Then I tiptoed into the kitchen. My parents sat on the porch, talking quietly. I grabbed two apples and combat-crawled back to my room. Then I stood on my bed, popped the screen off my window, and dropped to the ground behind the trailer.

My bike stood propped against the trailer's side. I walked it down the path to the forest, not looking behind me. Then I climbed on. Pinecones bounced under my tires, and gray squirrels scurried past me into trees. At our pond, I nearly ran over Eric.

"What're you doing here?" I asked.

He knelt with a shovel, digging in the soft black dirt. "I look for worms. What you doing?"

"Running away."

The words flew from my mouth before I could stop them. But once they were out, I knew they were true. I couldn't go back to California. My father would lose himself in his job again, and one day I'd find him dead. That would kill me. I'd head for the butte instead, live on the land like John Muir. My parents would have to return to Redondo Beach without me.

Eric stood up. A reddish-brown night crawler dangled from his fingers. The trees cast long shadows across the forest. Crows and blue jays were packing it in for the evening, making room for owls. "I go with you?"

I shook my head. "Bye, Eric. See you someday . . . maybe."

I pedaled through the forest behind the Millers' house and rode toward the road. The hill loomed ahead of me. I dropped my bike into the lowest gear and stood up on the pedals. "I will . . . make it . . . to the . . . top!" I panted in time with my pounding heart.

This time, I did.

I clicked into high gear and flew downtown. I stopped in front of the market. *Granola bars and soda.*

The can of Coke cooled my sweaty palms. The bald, tattooed cashier nodded at my backpack full of quarters and dimes. "Got quite a stash there." I ducked my head, sure he could tell I was a runaway.

"I'll take a couple of those, too." I pointed to the sugarcoated gummy worms in a plastic tub beside the register. The cashier wrapped them in tissue paper, and I stuffed them in my backpack.

Back outside, I sped toward Eyrie Road. The sky glowed navy blue with a thin line of pink in the west. Ahead of me, a short, stocky cyclist rode with so many red and white lights on his bike that he looked like a two-wheeled police car. He was a strong rider and fast. I finally caught him at a red light.

"Hi, Solo!"

"*Eric*? Where are you going?"

Eric gripped his handlebar in one hand and pulled a squirming pink night crawler out of his pocket. "I come with you. Feed the birds."

Until that instant, I didn't know exactly where I'd start my ascent to the butte. The Pig Wheel led me on the path it knew best—toward the raptor center. How had Eric known?

"Go home," I told him. "You're not invited."

Tears filled his eyes. "My father yell at my mother. I run away, too!"

In my head, I saw Mr. Miller's raised fist, felt his rasping breath hot against the back of my neck. I understood.

"Okay," I sighed, "but step on it. We gotta get out of town before someone sees us."

Eric pulled a red flashing light off his brake cable. "Put this on."

I clipped it to my bike. "Thanks."

We pedaled up Eyrie. Three deer burst from the bushes and stepped onto the road. Eric and I slowed to a stop, and he held up his magnifying glass. The mother deer pranced across the pavement, but her two fawns paused and stared at us, black tails twitching and big ears swiveling.

"Better get out of the road," I said, my voice too loud in the near silence of early evening.

The fawns bounded into the forest after their mother.

"Watch out for her," I muttered. "Parents equal chaos."

"I miss my mother." Eric's face glowed pale in the red light clipped to his jacket collar.

I looked at the sun dropping low over the firs. "Too late to go back."

"Yeah." He heaved a shuddering sigh and hunched over his handlebars. "I know."

CHAPTER SIXTEEN

OWLS CALL OUT THE NAMES OF PEOPLE WHO ARE ABOUT TO DIE

lang! A woman I'd never seen before rolled the gate across the raptor center's driveway and locked it around a post. "Must be another volunteer," I whispered to Eric.

We crouched in the trees and watched her car's brake lights disappear down the road. Then we climbed over the gate, hauling our bikes up after us. My pig hit metal and squeaked.

"Well?" Edgar called from her mew. But she didn't laugh.

Eric's eyes widened. "Who that?"

"Shh!" I hissed. "It's a crow."

I glanced up the driveway, half expecting Minerva to appear with her hands on her hips.

We're closed. What're you doing here on a Saturday night? I could hear her voice sharp in my ears.

But the driveway stood empty.

"We can hide our bikes here." I rolled the Pig Wheel behind a rickety storage shed. Eric slipped on the pine-needled path and crashed his bike against mine.

"Sorry, Solo."

The merlins shrieked. High above us, the bald eagles screeched. Now, owls began to hoot—their calls bounced off trees, echoing around us.

WHOO-hoo-oo-oo-oo-WHOO-WHOO!

Artemis's warning call.

I pulled Eric behind the shed. "Turn off your bike lights!" I hissed. "All of them!"

Footsteps crunched down the gravel path. Minerva's ears were as good as any owl's. She knew something didn't sound right.

"What is it, Edgar?" she asked from somewhere above us.

"Well . . ." Edgar said. "Well . . . ha ha ha ha!"

Eric giggled. I clapped my hand over his mouth. *"Hold your breath!"* I hissed.

He puffed out his cheeks and nodded.

Minerva walked down the driveway. The long white beam of her flashlight swooped through the night, just missing the toe of my hiking boot. She wore a robe, and a towel covered her hair like a turban. She stood with her back to us and shook her fist in the dark. "Leave my birds alone! And if you're dropping off another cat, this time leave a bag of cat food!"

She headed up toward her house. Eric's teeth chattered under my hand. "Mmmhngw," he said.

I pulled my hand away. "What?"

"I hungry."

"Here." I pulled the apples out of my backpack and opened the can of Coke under my jacket so the crack and fizz wouldn't give us away. I gave him the can and reached into my backpack. "Dessert." I held out the two gummy worms wrapped in paper.

"Those for birds." He put the gummy worms in his pocket.

Every time we crunched into our apples, I cringed and waited for the flashlight to blast into my eyes. If Minerva found us, what would she do? I'd be in a juvenile correctional facility by morning, and Eric would have to return to his father.

We had to get out of here before daylight.

The wind rose. Fluffy white clouds drifted across the moon. I put on my jacket and hugged my knees to my chest.

We could hike to the top of Spencer Butte and live in the woods until our parents stopped looking for us. Then we'd build a tree house. We'd scavenge for food, and I'd write screenplays on bark and leaves. I'd publish them under a pseudonym . . . John Muir.

Already, I had a good scene in my head.

FADE IN

EXTERIOR. DENTED OLD TRAILER IN FIELD SURROUNDED BY FOREST - DAY

INTERIOR. SMALL ABANDONED BEDROOM - DAY.

Yellowed surfing posters on the walls. A Darth Vader bank overturned and empty on the bed. MOM and DAD sit on the floor, weeping in each other's arms.

                    MOM
  We used to have a wonderful son. But
  we only thought about ourselves. And
  so he disappeared.

                    DAD
  I wish I'd spent more time with him.
  We could have gone hiking or biking,
  but now it's too late.

CLOSE-UP of a photograph in Dad's hand. A tear falls, smudging the picture of a black-haired kid in shorts and hiking boots.

FADE OUT

I closed my eyes. What was wrong with me? Two months ago, I would have been packed and waiting in the car to return to Redondo Beach.

Surfing is your bliss, remember? Don't you hate Oregon?

A yawn snuck up on me. I leaned against the shed, feeling my mind slow down.

People can have more than one bliss. Minerva said so.

I don't know how or when I fell asleep. I woke up to the sound of hooting—owls calling all around me. I recognized the frantic burble of screech owls, the Who-Cooks-for-You hoot of a barred owl, and the lower alarm call of a great horned owl.

"Eric?" I reached out in the dark to see if he'd fallen asleep, too.

No one sat beside me.

I leapt up. If Minerva found him, she'd ruin my plans. I stumbled on stiff legs through the trees. "Eric? Eric?" I whispered. "*Get back here!*"

I peered into the spotted owls' mew and heard the nervous clack of beaks in the dark.

"Sorry, girls."

I ran toward the screech owls, slipped, and fell backward into blackberries.

WHOO-hoo-oo-oo-oo-WHOO-WHOO! Artemis called.

I yanked vines off my legs. Thorns tore my skin; I barely felt them. Suddenly, I knew exactly where Eric was. The thought made me shiver with terror.

Some Native Americans believe that great horned owls cry out the names of people who are about to die.

"No!"

I raced up the path just as the moon slipped out from behind the clouds. It beamed down like a spotlight on Eric right as he turned the key forgotten in the padlock and walked into Artemis's mew.

CHAPTER SEVENTEEN
SOLO'S KRIYĀ

Artemis shrieked and soared across her mew, wings and legs outstretched. Huge feathered feet seized Eric's arm. Pain crumpled his face.

"Stop!" I shouted. I leapt inside and grabbed the leather jesses around Artemis's legs. She let go of Eric and pulled away from me, launching herself to the other end of the mew. I stumbled to the door and pushed Eric outside. Wings rushed toward my head. Talons raked my back like lightning bolts. A scream tore through the darkness.

My scream.

Artemis whirled and rushed toward me again. Just in time, I burst out of the mew and slammed the door behind me. The owl smacked into the wire. She dropped to the ground and lay still.

Oh, no! No! I have to go back in, try to save her.

But in the distance, a door slammed. Footsteps pounded toward us.

"*Run!*" I grabbed Eric and pushed him down the hill. We fell, ripping through blackberry vines to the dirt path below.

"Ouch," Eric whispered.

Above us, Minerva's flashlight swung wildly. "I know you're out there!" she yelled. "I'm calling the police!"

I clutched my ankle, barely feeling the sprain.

Is Artemis dead?

She'd hit the door hard enough to break her wings, or worse, her neck.

"Why'd you go in that mew?" I clutched Eric's arm.

"Wanna give the owl my worm."

He opened his hand, revealing a mangled gummy worm. A trickle of blood ran down his wrist. In the moonlight, I saw his shredded jacket sleeve.

I pulled him through the trees to a clearing hidden from the path. We leaned against a log. "Take off your jacket," I commanded. "Oh . . . *crap.*"

Eric's arm dripped blood from six gashes where Artemis's talons had dug in. "You gotta get to the hospital."

He shook his head. "I run away with you."

"You'll get hurt worse. Can you make it down the hill on your bike? You can call from the market at the bottom. I'm sorry, Eric," I whispered. "This is something I've gotta do myself."

"Solo." Eric moved so close that his nose almost touched mine. "You . . . not . . . alone." He spoke slowly, like he was trying to make me understand. "I . . . your . . . friend."

My throat stung. I took a deep, ragged breath.

"Okay. We'd better get going. Can you make it to the top?"

I helped Eric slip his jacket sleeve off one arm and tie it around his neck to make a sling.

"Solo? You hurt, too." He pointed to a dark stain on the log. I craned my neck to look over my shoulder. The back of my T-shirt hung in ribbons. I glimpsed bloody trails and gritted my teeth against the sudden searing pain.

Eric found the path and began to walk. I followed, stumbling on rocks and roots in the dark. My back throbbed and my ankle ached with every step. I talked to distract myself, babbling anything that popped into my head.

"When I moved here, I didn't even know what a raptor was," I mumbled. "Couldn't tell a hawk from a falcon. Last week, we got a sick kestrel in the clinic. I fed her by hand. Minerva says if her wing doesn't heal right, we'll keep her as company for the other kestrel. You should hear her squawk when she sees me come in with her morning mouse. I like kestrels better than owls—they're funny and friendly and . . ."

Suddenly, a wild great horned owl hooted above us. I ducked, and the gashes on my back seared with pain.

"Let's go!" I cried. We scrambled up the boulders, slipping on damp lichen.

At the top of the butte, the wind was blowing like crazy, howling through the trees. We climbed toward the pine tree we'd sat under with Mrs. Miller. "No picnic?" Eric panted.

I searched my jacket pockets for the granola bars I'd stashed. "The rest of my food must've fallen out."

We hunched down behind two boulders, trying to block the wind. The sky spread over us, speckled with stars. At last, my heartbeat slowed. I gulped cold air like water.

Eric cupped his ears with his hands. "I hear stars."

I snorted. "Stars don't make a sound!"

Still, I listened, trying to hear what Eric heard. All I could make out were the frogs and crickets holding a choir rehearsal in the bushes.

"Falling star!" Eric pointed.

"Where?"

I followed his finger to a white flash across the sky. "Aren't we supposed to wish on it?"

Eric nodded. "I wish I have cookies. What about you?"

I wish . . . I wish Artemis wasn't dead.

Eric hugged his arm to his side and jabbered something about a meteor shower. "The Perseid shower. We got good seats."

He was right. We sat there against the boulders and watched meteors shoot across the sky like our own private screening of *Star Wars*. For a while, I tried to wish on every one.

I wish for Artemis to be okay.
I wish for Eric to be okay.
I wish for Mom and Dad . . .
What *did* I wish for my parents?

Minerva said she'd called the police. Would they find us, and would Mom and Dad tell them to throw me in jail for running away?

How could I explain that I didn't really hate my father? That sometimes you can love somebody so much, but you can't live with him anymore, watching him give in to the dark side?

I wish for Dad to be okay.

Eric yawned. "I sleepy."

I examined his arm. Blood had seeped through his jacket and dried to a crust on the fabric. "Take a nap. I'll keep a lookout." I knotted our jacket sleeves together in case he decided to take another hike.

"I stay awake," he said, but in a minute, he was snoring.

I sat there shivering, staring up at the stars. Was this what Minerva meant by a *kriyā*—a spiritual emergency? Any second, the police could haul me to jail for going AWOL, for kidnapping a disabled boy I'd once shot, for murdering an owl.

Mr. Miller was right. I *was* a criminal.

Tears burned my face—tears that had been locked deep inside. They'd refused to come out even when I'd seen my father stretched on the hospital bed with tubes sticking out of his nose and mouth and I tried to hold his hand but he turned his head to the wall so he wouldn't have to see me. Now, they poured hot down my cheeks, twin waterfalls of sorrow.

"Artemis didn't mean to hurt you, Eric." I wiped my nose on my sleeve.

Eric snored, but I kept talking. "Okay . . . well . . . maybe she did . . . but don't take it personally. She's a wild animal. She thought you were invading her territory. How would you like it if someone threatened a place you loved?"

I stared down at the gummy worm clutched in Eric's hand. "Artemis is a beautiful bird . . . she's smart and powerful, and . . ."

My words floated off into the wind, and I fell asleep.

Chapter Eighteen

THAT OWL MUST BE DESTROYED

A h-choo!"

"Bless you," I whispered.

Beside me, Eric groaned. Even through a fog of dreams, I could tell his arm hurt. My own body ached with cold.

Slowly, I opened my eyes. The sky above the trees glowed pink. In the half light, bushes and rocks made shadowy silhouettes. I squinted at a figure with a backpack below us, slowly making his way to where we sat.

An early morning hiker? Some evil dude eyeing my backpack full of quarters and dimes? My fingers inched out and clutched one strap.

The man kept climbing, straight toward us.

I poked Eric in the side. "Wake up!" I hissed in his ear.

What if he was a kidnapper? If he tried to grab us, we could leap off the rocks and roll to the field below.

I could get away. Could Eric?

Eric opened one eye. "Breakfast?" he mumbled.

My eyes locked on the man. He sprang toward me, and I yelled.

"Dad!"

In an instant, I blew my cover and any hope of running away. My father stood in front of us clutching a bunch of bananas and a bag of cookies.

"Solo." He dropped to the dirt beside me. Warm hands cupped my cheeks. "Oh my God, son. I thought you were . . . Minerva heard a commotion in an owl's mew and found your bike. Are you hurt?"

I bit my lip to keep from confessing. One look at the talon marks on my back, and he'd know who'd killed Artemis. But now Eric was wide awake, too, eyes glued to the bag of cookies.

"Solo's back hurt," he told my father.

I tried to shrug. "It's nothing."

Too late. Dad walked behind me and gasped. "What the . . ."

Carefully, he peeled away a piece of my T-shirt. I ground my teeth as cloth tore away from raw skin.

"We've gotta get you to a doctor." He draped his jacket over my shoulders. "Put this on and zip it up." He pulled two blankets from the backpack. "Wrap yourselves in these, boys. You're lucky it was a warm night."

"Ouch." Eric clutched the blanket tight around his neck. Dad shot a question into my eyes.

"He's hurt, too," I mumbled.

My father examined Eric's bloody arm. "His parents are going to want an explanation. They're waiting down at the raptor center."

I nodded, miserable. What was the point of trying to keep secrets if Artemis was dead? The minute Minerva saw our injuries, she'd know who'd been in the mew.

Dad gave Eric the bag of cookies. "You look hungry, young man."

His voice rang out solid and strong. I stole a glance at him. He sucked in big gulps of the cool morning air. The pink sky deepened to orange, and birds began to chirp in the trees around us. "We'd better head back," he said.

Back to California, away from this place.

Good-bye, butte.

I peered into the sky, hoping to spot the bald eagle again.

Nothing.

My father helped us down the boulders. Eric didn't cry. He just held tight to his cookies. My stomach growled, but I couldn't eat the banana Dad offered. My guts churned like a storm-tossed ocean.

"Your mother's at the raptor center, too," he told me. "Quite a place you've got there."

I don't have any place.

I stumbled behind him down the switchbacks. Finally, we turned and climbed the steep path to the center. A knot of people stood on the lawn. I untangled them, searching for the police. Mrs. Miller . . . Mom . . . Minerva . . . Lucas and Leah holding hands.

Leah spotted us first. She rushed over and hugged me. Pain shot up my back, and I bit down on my tongue to keep from crying.

"I told you they'd gone camping!" she said to Lucas.

Sergeant Bird Nerd tried to scowl, but it didn't work. "It's good to see you two," he sighed.

My mother threw her arms around me. "You could have been killed!" Her eyes looked teary and bloodshot. Her hair hung limp, and a worried crack jutted between her eyebrows like a fault line. She looked awful.

Beside me, Mrs. Miller hugged Eric. "See, y'all? I told you they just went on a little overnight." But her hands shook as she clutched him to her chest.

Minerva draped another blanket around Eric's shoulders and handed me one. I searched her eyes for news of Artemis. She peered back at me, her face grim.

Mr. Miller stalked down the hill, coming from the direction of the great horned owl's mew. In spite of two jackets and two blankets, a chill prickled my spine. He hovered over us in his long black trench coat.

"What happened to your arm?" he rasped and caught hold of Eric's bloody wrist.

Eric blinked at me. "I fall down the hill," he said. "Solo save me."

Did he lie on purpose, or had he already forgotten what had happened?

Mr. Miller's face froze in a mask of rage. He dropped a chewed-up gummy worm into Minerva's hand. "I found *this* outside that owl's cage."

Minerva pinned me under her gaze.

"We didn't mean to kill her . . . honest," I whispered.

But what was the point of arguing? Jail seemed inevitable.

Mr. Miller untied the jacket sling and tore fabric from the gashes in Eric's arm. He unclenched his teeth just long enough to let loose five words—words that pierced my heart, and from the look on Minerva's face, pierced hers, too.

"That owl must be destroyed."

Lucas and Leah stared at Mr. Miller. Mom gripped Dad's arm.

"No."

Minerva stepped toward Mr. Miller. She stood a good six inches shorter than he did, but I swear she looked him right in the eye. "Artemis has a right to defend her own life. Raptors protect their territory."

"Protect it from whom?" Mr. Miller growled.

Minerva's words hung in the air so clearly I could almost see them.

From people like you.

But she never got to speak them because my father grabbed my hand. "I'd like to see this owl, Solo."

Eric nodded. "I feed her my worm!"

I hung my head. Again, I heard the thud of the bird's body against the mew door. *Artemis is dead, and it's all my fault.*

But now everyone rushed up the gravel path toward the mews. Even Mr. Miller stumbled along, sandwiched between me and my father, and Lucas and Leah. Eric led the way, wrapped in blankets.

We crowded in front of Artemis's mew. Her perch stood empty.

Minerva stepped in front of us and spread her arms, warning us away. "She's feeling territorial today. Leave her alone!"

Feeling territorial . . . today?

"Artemis is alive?"

"I'm going to get my shotgun." Mr. Miller turned, but Eric grabbed the sleeve of his coat and held on.

"You hafta see the owl," he insisted.

That's when I got the idea. People hate what they don't understand. I'd despised Oregon and owls and even Eric until I began to see them in a different way.

If Artemis had any hope of surviving Mr. Miller's wrath, she had to show herself.

I pushed through the crowd and grabbed the hose. Lucas read my mind and ran to turn on the spigot.

I aimed the hose toward the perch. The water sprayed out cold and silvery in the early morning light.

No owl.

Leah clasped her hands. "Be patient."

I arched the hose, spraying mist onto the gravel. Beside me, Lucas hooted softly.

WHOO-hoo-oo-oo-oo-WHOO-WHOO!

Come on, Artemis. Please . . .

And then, with a magnificent flap of wings, the owl rose up to her perch. Her yellow eyes shifted from one face to another, finally landing on mine. I danced the water around her, over the jutting ear tufts, the soft brown and white feathers. She spread her wings wide. Her white chest flashed as she called to me.

WHOO-hoo-oo-oo-oo-WHOO-WHOO!

"See. She's beautiful!" I said, barely above a whisper.

Eric pulled the magnifying glass from around his neck and pushed it into his father's hand.

"She's a menace!" he growled.

Then something inside me snapped, like rubber bands that had been stretched around my heart. I felt them go zipping off into space.

"She's *not* a menace!" I yelled. "She's an incredible bird. You can't kill her!"

Eric stepped in front of the mew and glared at his father with the same look he'd shot Missing Tooth before he kicked him in the jaw. "Don't hurt this bird!"

"Here." I gave Eric the hose. "Aim this toward Artemis, and see what happens. She loves to take a shower."

As Eric sprayed her, Artemis lifted one shining brown wing and then the other, blissfully unaware that her life was in danger. A smile spread across Eric's face.

"Solo tell me owls have binocular eyes," he said. "And lopsided ears."

"Well?" Edgar said from her mew. "Ha ha ha ha!"

If this had been one of my screenplay scenes, everyone would have laughed and forgotten all about killing owls. But only my father chuckled.

Mom leaned over to whisper in his ear. "That's Edgar Allen Crow."

Then Dad really let loose, a laugh you could have heard clear at the top of the butte. "Edgar Allen Crow!" He slapped his thigh. "That's a good one!"

Mr. Miller stared at him. "You really are," he said slowly, "as crazy as they say."

Then he turned to Eric. For an instant, he seemed to actually see his son. He turned and stalked down the hill. "I've gotta get to the airport."

The rest of us huddled together, shielding Artemis. Mrs. Miller's cheeks burned red as her husband's car rumbled down the driveway. "Maybe it's better this way," she murmured to my mother. Then she kissed the top of my head. "Thank you for taking care of Eric, honey. You're a real live hero."

"He *is* a hero. He saved Artemis." Leah pulled something from her pocket and placed it around my neck. A beaded necklace with a silver feather charm, just like Lucas's. "I've got one, too," she said. "We made mine and one for you after we released the owl at the beach."

Lucas reached for the feather around his own neck and tugged it thoughtfully. "That guy can't really have Artemis killed, can he?"

"Absolutely not," Minerva snapped. "It's *illegal* for children to be in the raptor enclosures without an adult."

Here it came. My jail sentence.

My hands shook. I stuffed them into the pockets of Dad's jacket.

Good-bye, Leah. Good-bye, Lucas.

Lucas squeezed Leah's hand, then walked over to me. Quietly, he held out his arm and tapped the three white scars on his wrist. Then, I understood. He was the tough guy who'd once gone into Artemis's mew and gotten attacked.

"From At-Risk Youth to Sergeant Bird Nerd." He winked at me. "Heard you telling Artemis about my nickname."

Minerva walked over and bent to my eye level. "Our new volunteer called me at midnight. She said she accidentally left the key in Artemis's padlock."

She nodded toward Eric. "I think you saved someone else besides our owl."

Her eyes pierced mine. "I ran away once, too, Solo. Then I came here and started the raptor center. What will you start?"

How did she know I had been running away?

Mrs. Miller patted Eric's hand. "I'm gonna get this young man over to the hospital. I don't think he'll need stitches, but we'll just make real sure. You coming?"

My mom looked at me.

"I don't need to go to the hospital," I muttered. "I'm fine."

"Even so," Mom said, "I'd like to get some medicine on those cuts of yours and get you into warm clothes."

Dad jangled his keys. "Let's go," he said.

My parents couldn't wait to get out of here. I stared down at my filthy, bloody legs.

Good-bye, Edgar. Good-bye, Artemis.

Leah rustled a paper bag. "Hey, guys. I've got cookies for you."

Eric clapped his hands, winced at the pain in his arm, and grabbed the bag anyway. "More cookies!"

So he got his wish, the wish he'd made on the falling star. And I got mine. Artemis was okay. Eric was okay. Even my father was okay. The only one who wasn't okay was me.

What would I start? Nothing at all.

I closed my eyes, blocking out my parents and Minerva, the birds and my friends. Everything in my life felt like one huge bad ending.

CHAPTER NINETEEN
HOME

G ood-bye, Solo."
Minerva pushed a bag of gauze pads through
The Big Grape's sliding door and handed me a
bottle. "Antiseptic. For your back."

I slumped on the ripped bench seat and closed
my eyes.

"Hang in there," she whispered.

Outside the VW, she spoke with my parents. Lucas
and Leah stood beside Edgar's mew, talking quietly. My
body throbbed with pain. Even my soul hurt.

Mom hoisted the Pig Wheel into the back of the bus
and climbed into the driver's seat. My father climbed in
back and put an arm around me. "It's gonna be okay," he
said softly.

The Big Grape choked to a start. Mom pulled away
from the center with its dozens of mews, its flower gar-
dens, and the treatment room full of injured birds that
someone else would care for now that I was gone. The
black and white kitten peeked out at me from behind

the clinic's screen door. Someone else would get to take her home.

I watched through the back window as the center grew smaller and smaller. The lump in my throat swelled bigger and bigger. I pressed a fist into my gut.

Dad ruffled my hair. "Your mother and I had a marathon discussion last night when we couldn't find you. You know, Solo, eventually you've got to stop running and commit to a place."

My stomach went belly-up. An At-Risk Youth, and now a runaway. Would they commit me to juvenile corrections here, or would they wait till we got back to California?

"We're going to go to family counseling," Mom said.

"And I'm going separately once a week," my father added. "It's not a panacea, but it's a step in the right direction."

"Panacea?" I mumbled.

"He means a cure." Mom pulled a Snickers bar from her purse and tossed it to me. "I thought you could use this." She smiled at me in the rearview mirror. "Hey, don't expect me to give up the no sugar rule. This is a treat."

Dad caught my eye and winked. I stared back at him dully.

"I'm looking for part-time work at a bookstore," he said. "It'll give my day some structure and"—he reached to put a hand on Mom's shoulder—"help with finances."

"You'll get inspiration from all those books," she said. "We'll have wonderful stories to tell over dinner."

Their words rolled off me and away. I stared out the window at the green smear of firs and fields. *I never even got to pick blackberries. Now I never will, since we're moving.*

"Solo, did you hear me? I asked if you'd seen Minerva's bumper sticker."

"Why?"

"It said, FOLLOW YOUR BLISS. Isn't that wonderful?"

"Follow your bliss," Dad repeated slowly. "Good advice, isn't it, son? Minerva said she'd let me take a volunteer shift of my own . . . that is if you . . ."

Sometimes a raptor comes into the center so injured that all it can do is look at you—devastated eyes glittering from a ragged pile of feathers. I barely had the energy to blink at my parents through my tangled hair.

My father looked into my eyes. "Solo, we can stay."

"Stay?"

"If you want to. Otherwise, we can go back to California. It's not too late for either decision."

"What would *you* prefer?" Mom asked me.

What would *I* prefer?

Minerva was right: a person can have more than one bliss.

"I want to stay," I whispered.

My mother turned in the driveway and gunned The Big Grape toward our tin can trailer. A red-tailed hawk looked down at us from our telephone pole. Songbirds erupted in a tiny brown explosion from the feeder I'd hung in a cherry tree.

My father jumped out and scooped Mom into his arms. Laughing, he carried her up the porch steps and through the front door.

Then I knew we were home, for good.

FADE OUT

ACKNOWLEDGMENTS

No writer ever truly works alone on a book. I'm grateful to my husband, Jonathan, who inspired me to volunteer at our local raptor center after inviting me out on a date to pick up six hundred pounds of frozen rats and a live baby barred owl. Thank you to my agent, Jennifer Unter, for believing in this manuscript, and to Julie Matysik and Adrienne Szpyrka at Sky Pony for their insight as editors. I'm grateful for help from Gail Udell, Sarah Howery Hart, and George Estreich regarding Eric's speech patterns. A special thank you to the staff and volunteers at raptor centers across the world—they dedicate their lives to helping injured and orphaned birds of prey. And much gratitude to the raptors themselves, who bring good tidings and Nature's peace.

RESOURCES FOR RAPTOR LOVERS

Nonfiction Books

Adopted by an Owl: The True Story of Jackson the Owl by Robbyn Smith van Frankenhuyzen

Birds: Internet Linked by Gillian Doherty

Birds of Prey by Karen Stray Nolting and Jonathan P. Latimer

Eyewitness: Eagles & Birds of Prey by Jemima Parry-Jones

Owl Puke: The Book by Jane Hammerslough

Raptor! A Kid's Guide to Birds of Prey by Christyna M. Laubach, René Laubach, and Charles W. G. Smith

Fiction Books

Flyaway by Hellen Landolf

Frightful's Mountain by Jean Craighead George

Guardians of Ga'hoole by Kathryn Lasky

Hoot by Carl Hiaasen

There's an Owl in the Shower by Jean Craighead George

Websites

Hawkwatch International is a nonprofit dedicated to preserving raptors and their habitat: www.hawkwatch.org/

International Wildlife Rehabilitation Council is a great site for education and resources for wildlife conservation: http://theiwrc.org/

National Wildlife Rehabilitators Association provides links to finding a wildlife/raptor rehabilitator near you: www.nwrawildlife.org/content/finding-rehabilitator

The Peregrine Fund is a nonprofit working to conserve birds of prey: www.peregrinefund.org

RESOURCES ABOUT DOWN SYNDROME

Nonfiction Books

Count Us In: Growing up with Down Syndrome by Jason Kingsley and Mitchell Levitz

Riding the Bus with My Sister: A True Life Journey by Rachel Simon

The Shape of the Eye: A Memoir by George Estreich

Fiction Books

Dead Ends by Erin Jade Lange

Dear Blue Sky by Mary Sullivan

Dear America: Down the Rabbit Hole by Susan Campbell Bartoletti

Websites

Global Down Syndrome Foundation:
www.globaldownsyndrome.org/

National Association for Down Syndrome:
www.nads.org/

National Down Syndrome Society: www.ndss.org/

ABOUT THE AUTHOR

Melissa Hart loves hiking, kayaking, and camping with her husband and daughter throughout Oregon. She's the author of two books for adults—*Wild Within: How Rescuing Owls Inspired a Family,* and *Gringa: A Contradictory Girlhood.* She teaches high school literature for Laurel Springs, a distance-learning K-12 school, and for Whidbey Island's MFA in Creative Writing program. See more of her work, including her essays about owls and about her brother with Down syndrome at www.melissahart.com.